D1740215

The Quiet Day
The Commitment
Paperback Copyright © 2021 Lorhainne Ekelund
Editor: Talia Leduc

ISBN-13: 9781989698778

Give feedback on the book at:
lorhainneeckhart@hotmail.com

Twitter: @LEckhart
Facebook: AuthorLorhainneEckhart

Printed in the U.S.A

THE QUIET DAY

The O'Connells

LORHAINNE ECKHART

About the O'Connells

The O'Connells of Livingston, Montana, are not your typical family. Follow them on their journey to the dark and dangerous side of love in a series of romantic thrillers you won't want to miss. Raised by a single mother after their father's mysterious disappearance eighteen years ago, the six grown siblings live in a small town with all kinds of hidden secrets, lies, and deception. Much like the contemporary family romance series focusing on the Friessens, this romantic suspense series follows the lives of the O'Connell family as each of the siblings searches for love.

The O'Connells

The Neighbor
The Third Call
The Secret Husband
The Quiet Day
The Commitment, An O'Connell Novella
The Missing Father
The Hometown Hero

Justice
The Family Secret
The Fallen O'Connell
The Return of the O'Connells
And The She Was Gone
The Stalker
The O'Connell Family Christmas
The Girl Next Door
Broken Promises
The Gatekeeper

The O'Connells Box Set Collections

The O'Connells Books 1 - 3
The O'Connells Books 4 - 6
The O'Connells Books 7 - 9
The O'Connells Books 10 - 12

The Quiet Day

As a female firefighter in a small town, Suzanne O'Connell knows that every day will go one of two ways: Either nothing happens, or she suddenly finds herself in over her head. Firefighters never, ever say the words "It's a quiet day!"—because that's when all hell breaks loose, and their peaceful, easy day suddenly turns into their worst nightmare. This is exactly what happens to Suzanne when she finds herself trapped with Harold Waters, local law enforcement officer and her old flame, and fellow fireman Toby Chandler, who, according to everyone, is the kind of guy you want watching your back.

In an unusual turn of events, the stakes turn deadly, and Suzanne discovers that trusting the wrong man could leave her life hanging in the balance.

Chapter 1

"You going to eat that entire tub of ice cream, or do the rest of us get to have some?" Marcus said as he strode into his kitchen, where Suzanne was sitting alone after rummaging through his freezer for the ice cream she'd brought over. She just stared at him as she jabbed a large tablespoon into the big tub of strawberry swirl again and lifted out a big hunk.

"Help yourself," she said around the mouthful, feeling the brain freeze the minute she swallowed.

Marcus shook his head, taking the tub of ice cream from her and moving it near the sink, away from her. He reached for three bowls from the cupboard, and Suzanne leaned against the nicked-up blue and white counter. Marcus and Charlotte's house was small, dated. The kitchen was closed off from the rest of the house, and the old wood floor squeaked in places, but it had a big yard and was close to their mom's place, and Eva had her own bedroom.

Suzanne could hear the voices of her family coming

from the small living room as she took another bite from the hunk of ice cream still on her spoon.

"So why are you hiding out in here?" Marcus said with only a glance over his shoulder. He was in a faded army green T-shirt and blue jeans, sock-footed, and his dark wavy hair appeared freshly cut. He also seemed very much at home, the family man with an instant family, a role she hadn't expected for him. Six-year-old Eva came running into the kitchen in a red and white flowered T-shirt and pajama pants and wrapped her arms around his leg, standing on his foot.

"Can I have ice cream, please...?" she said. She was so damn sweet and tiny.

Marcus smiled down at her and rustled her shoulder-length brown hair, also freshly cut. Suzanne recalled that her mom had booked a "granddaughters hair day" for Eva and Alison only the day before at Delilah's Hair, a friend's salon.

"Just dishing yours up now, sweet pea," Marcus said as he lifted her and sat her on the counter. Suzanne loved the nickname he had given her. "Here, you can help," he continued and gave Eva the scoop, his hand over hers.

Suzanne finished off the ice cream on her spoon, holding it up. Her cell phone was silent, its screen still black, and she double checked to see if the thing was powered on.

"You didn't answer me, Suzanne. What's going on?" Marcus asked as he helped Eva down and handed her a bowl. She walked with it back into the living room, all smiles.

"You sure are good with her," Suzanne said, then gestured toward him with her spoon. "You given any thought to what will happen when her mom is released from prison?"

Marcus was still dishing ice cream into three other bowls, and he let out a sigh before shaking his head. "You're changing the subject—and that's a long ways off, not something I'm worrying about right now or putting on the table for discussion. So what's up with you? Because you're off tonight. How come, problems?" He gestured with the empty scoop to her and the cell phone she was holding, and she forced herself to put it down on the counter.

She shook her head. "No, everything's fine," she said, not sure what to make of his face and the way he was looking at her.

"Bullshit, Suzanne. You're usually way better at hiding your off-ness, so what's got you so glued to that phone? You've been texting someone, and all I can figure is whoever it is has you kind of distracted. You've barely said anything to anyone, just glanced at your phone every thirty seconds. This isn't like you. Then you slipped off alone to the kitchen, eating away your stress, as Charlotte says."

She hadn't realized he'd been watching. She had to fight the urge to pick up her phone, to look again at the texts that had gone unanswered.

"The silent treatment?" Marcus let out a sarcastic laugh.

"It's nothing, really," Suzanne said. "And I wasn't stress eating," she added for effect.

He turned around, tossed the scoop in the sink, and wiped his hands on a dishtowel before gesturing to the ice cream lid, which was still beside her on the counter. "Whatever you say, Suzanne."

She reached for it and crossed the kitchen to hand it to him, just shaking her head when he gestured as if asking whether she wanted more. He had a way of making her seem defensive when she was anything but.

"Just for the record, Suzanne, you can keep telling me it's nothing, but I know it isn't, or you wouldn't be so distracted. You may as well just save us all the aggravation and tell me." He was still leaning on the counter and didn't look as if he were leaving anytime soon.

"Fine, you want to know? It's just someone who hasn't answered me, is all. We kind of had plans, and then…" She shrugged.

His expression darkened. "Please tell me we're not talking about that asshole, Toby."

There it was, exactly why she hadn't wanted to say anything.

"Tell me how you really feel, Marcus." She was still holding the empty spoon and thought of the tub of ice cream she'd been drowning her sorrows in moments earlier. Yup, she could definitely have used another scoop —but it wasn't stress eating, because she didn't do that.

"Well, I'll take that as my answer," he said in a tone that bothered her. "What the hell are you doing, Suzanne? You can do so much better. He's got nothing going for him. He doesn't have a sincere bone in his body, and that phony plastic smile he gives to everyone…shallow, no depth at all. If I really have to dig to find something redeeming about the guy, that should tell you something. I mean, why him? I don't understand why you'd do that to yourself."

She had to fight the urge to roll her shoulders as he went on. At the same time, she wasn't too inclined to share anything about her reasoning. The chemistry she had with Toby didn't happen with just any guy.

"You're being overdramatic, Marcus. Toby is a good guy."

Marcus just shook his head, and the look he tossed her said he didn't agree. She knew there was no love lost there, though the dislike was one sided. Her brother had never made any excuses for how he felt about Toby, but Toby had never said the same about him.

"Really? How about the fact that he's also your boss now, even though you trained him? Doesn't that get to you even just a little bit, Suzanne? Because it should." Marcus lifted the bowls of ice cream, already jabbed with spoons, and stepped over to her.

She had to remind herself that Marcus knew which of her emotional buttons to push. She pulled in a breath and forced herself to look away, then back to him. "That wasn't on Toby. You should know that. Can I blame him for wanting the lieutenant job?" She shrugged, trying to put some lightness in her tone.

She didn't want to admit that she still felt as if the rug had been yanked out from under her, considering she'd expected the promotion and had deserved it, yet when it happened, she realized she hadn't even been considered. She pulled in another breath and took in the way Marcus was still watching her as if waiting for her reaction.

"Yeah, you can, Suzanne, and you should. He didn't earn it, and he doesn't appreciate you. You dating him?"

There it was, the million-dollar question of just how committed Toby was to her. What could she say?

"It's not that serious, you know—and how is this any of your business, anyway?"

Marcus took another step toward her, but before he could reply, Charlotte stepped into the kitchen.

"Hey," she said. "Was wondering what was taking you so long. Alison is asking for her ice cream, since Eva is already done. Did I walk in on something?" Her long dark hair was hanging loose. Suzanne swore she could make anything look stunning, including the faded jeans and old T-shirt of Marcus's that she wore now. Some women just had that amazing, sexy, curvy appeal, but Suzanne never had.

She watched as Charlotte slid her hand around Marcus's waist, and he handed one of the bowls to her. Suzanne hoped her envy didn't show. He pressed a kiss to Charlotte's lips—and, damn, their closeness was uncomfortable. She wished they wouldn't do that right when they were having a conversation.

"No, nothing, just Suzanne mooning over Toby," Marcus said. "Let me guess: You've texted or called, and he hasn't called you back?" The way he was including Charlotte in this private conversation only added salt to her wound.

Here she was, lonely on a Saturday night when she'd wanted—no, expected to be out with Toby. They had plans, she assumed, but maybe not. She was now questioning what they had actually agreed on. Was she misreading things? She hated feeling like she was assuming something in whatever this was between them.

Charlotte seemed to hesitate as she gave everything to Suzanne, who now felt as if her personal life had taken center stage, out in the open for everyone to scrutinize. That was something she didn't want.

"I texted. He must be busy," she said. Even as it fell from her lips, she knew it sounded pathetic. It was unlike her to make excuses for anyone. Her brother only grunted, and Charlotte winced.

"He's blowing you off," Marcus said. "More than likely, he's with someone else. You ever thought of that?"

Then her cell phone dinged, and she practically landed on it, seeing a text from Toby.

Sorry, babe. Got hung up. How about my place in an hour?

She held the phone in front of her, feeling excitement or something. When Marcus rested his hand over the phone, she thought he was going to take it from her. As she lifted her gaze to her brother's, his expression was anything but friendly.

"Please do not be one of those girls," he said. Then he stepped away, inclining his head and glancing toward Charlotte and the bowl of ice cream she was holding before walking out of the kitchen. She could hear him calling Alison.

Charlotte gave everything to Suzanne. "Don't mind Marcus. He just loves you, is all, and doesn't want to see some guy messing with you, considering how he feels about Toby."

Of course, she didn't want to hear that, especially from Charlotte. Maybe that was why she felt so on edge as she pulled in another breath, realizing she was still gripping her spoon.

"Thanks, but Marcus is just sticking his nose where it doesn't belong, and he's way off base with Toby. Anyway, as I said, it's not serious. It's just a thing." She shrugged, feeling the bitterness in the way the words rolled off her tongue. She couldn't put a label on this thing happening between her and Toby. Yeah, she really liked him, but it seemed the effort was entirely on her side.

Charlotte must have known, as she just offered a smile and lifted her hands in a gesture Suzanne hoped meant she'd leave it alone and not offer an opinion. "You know, I'm not too sure about Marcus being off base, Suzanne. One thing I know about your brother is how well he reads everyone, better than most—and Toby, he's a player. Just watch yourself, because from where I'm sitting, I can see that Toby is possibly stringing you along. When he texts you and tells you to come running, you may want to ask him who he was with before you."

Before Suzanne could set her straight, Charlotte rested

her hand on her arm and walked out of the kitchen. Then her phone dinged.

Let me know if you're coming, Toby wrote, and he added two flirty emojis that would've been cute if she hadn't just had Charlotte and Marcus insinuate that Toby wasn't being straight with her.

The problem was that they just didn't know him.

As she dumped her spoon into the sink, still holding her phone, she saw the three dots that meant he was sending another text, but she was reminded of Charlotte's words. Where had he been, and what had happened to their plan of grabbing a few beers, going out together? Now, he was two hours late.

Chapter 2

Suzanne's cell phone rang from where it was stashed on the passenger seat with her purse as she worked the clutch in her seventies classic MGB, which would likely always be a work in progress. In fact, she'd just replaced the clutch, a part that wasn't exactly stocked at the local auto shop, given her car's age. The canvas top was up, and she was still smarting over how Charlotte and Marcus had come at her over Toby as if she were a teenager who didn't know any better. What business was it of theirs, anyway? Why couldn't they see that Toby was a great guy?

And why hadn't she bothered to respond to his text? It had made her feel like she was an afterthought, but that was ridiculous, because she was...what?

She was going to surprise him, she told herself. Maybe that was the reason for the sick feeling in the pit of her stomach. Doubts were something she'd never allowed to get stuck in her head, but her brother and his live-in girl-friend had just alluded to the possibility that Toby wasn't as into her as she was into him, and that was so off base!

She dragged the stick and heard the grind as she changed gears too fast. Her cell phone started ringing again, and when she glanced over to the lit-up screen and saw it was Toby, she considered for only a second before pressing the green icon and holding the phone to her ear.

"I'm on my way," she started, balancing the phone between her shoulder and ear so she could shift gears again.

"Was wondering, since I didn't hear from you. Was about to give up and head out."

Seriously? She actually pulled the phone away and stared at it for a second as she pulled up and stopped at a set of lights that had turned red. She put the phone back to her ear, her hand ready to shift gears again.

"You're going out?" she said. There it was, that feeling she hadn't been able to shake. "What's going on, Toby? I thought you and I were supposed to go for drinks, but then you didn't respond to any of my texts. Now, after how long, I suddenly get one from you telling me to come on over? Thought it was time for the two of us to date in public. We are dating, right…?"

She heard the sigh on the other end and could sense some brush-off coming.

"You're reading too much into things," he said. "Sorry I didn't respond, but I was held up, unavoidable. Comes with the title, you know. But you know what else, Suzanne? This is starting to feel like you're giving me the third degree when all I want to do is stay in tonight. Didn't realize we had plans set in stone. You didn't respond to my text, so what am I to think? Come on, don't push so hard…" There he went, sounding pissed when she was the one who should've been.

"Not so much set in stone," she said, "but we were going out."

She wasn't sure what sound he made on the other end, considering the purr of the engine wasn't exactly quiet. The light turned green, and she gave it gas and had to juggle the phone between her shoulder and ear again.

"Look, how about I cook dinner?" Toby said. "I'm hungry. Maybe you haven't eaten? I'll whip up a batch of linguini for us. What do you say?"

Dinner, just her and Toby…and, of course, what would follow but sex? Hot sex. Then she'd go home, because they were still at that stage of not staying over.

There they were again, those doubts from her brother and Charlotte. Damn them, already!

"Well, I suppose dinner would be nice," she said.

"That's great," he said. "Hey, listen, since you're on your way, would you mind stopping at the store and picking up a package of linguini noodles? And garlic, too, since I'm out. Oh, and looks like I'm out of tomatoes for a sauce, too. Why don't you grab one of those premade jars of linguini sauce, as well, and I can whip up a salad to go with?"

She was sure he was rummaging through a cupboard or fridge, and she was stuck on the fact that she was now picking up groceries. "So instead of going out, you're making me dinner…yet I'm picking dinner up. Really?" She didn't even try to dial back the sarcasm in her tone.

"Well, I just thought since you're already out…"

"Fine, never mind," she said. "I'm just giving you a hard time. I'll stop and pick up dinner so you can make it for me and hide me away at your place, alone, and not be seen in public."

"I'll make it up to you—and I have some news to share, too. You'll be happy for me…" he drawled in that sexy voice of his, the one that could get her to do anything. At least he had eased her confusion from seconds ago. Damn

Marcus, anyway, for getting in her head. She was better than that.

"Fine, I'll stop at the box store and should be there in about fifteen," she said. "Can't wait to see you."

She could see the store just up ahead as she geared down, then realized as soon as she hung up, just as a smile touched her lips, that he'd initially said he was about to go out, then that he wanted to stay in—and he'd never corrected her about not wanting to be seen as an item in public.

So he had news, what news? What was it with Toby? At times he seemed so elusive, all over the place and all about himself.

There it was again, that seed of doubt from her brother that just wouldn't get out of her head.

She pulled into the parking lot and into a spot beside a black pickup, then stepped out of her car and gave the heavy door a shove closed with a squeak. She slid her key into the lock and headed in.

Way too many choices. She found herself grabbing two jars of marinara sauce, pasta, and what else did he need? Garlic, right. But there was already some in the sauce, so…

"Suzanne, almost didn't recognize you."

It was his voice, so deep that it pulled her abruptly from her distraction. She found herself looking over to Harold Waters, in a deputy uniform much like her brother's, but from the next county over. His blond hair was short and tidy, not something she remembered, but he still had that perpetually pissed-off expression that reminded her how much of an absolute asshole he was. He dragged his gaze over her, and she had to fight the urge to slap him.

"Like what you see?" She inclined her head, holding the basket of groceries and resting her hand on her hip, still in her blue uniform, having not changed since work. His basket was filled with steak, chips, nachos, and milk. She dragged her own gaze up and over him in the same manner. It was then she thought she spotted an edge, something in the pull of his lips, not a smile.

All he did was grunt, taking his time before answering. "You look good," he said. "Guess I don't have to ask what you've been up to. Thought I heard you joined the fire department."

She wasn't sure what to make of the way he'd said it. There was just something about Harold that she'd never been able to figure out. He had a way of giving her everything when he was talking to her.

"Excuse me," a woman said, and Harold gestured to Suzanne, moving her out of the way as if they were together, barely glancing over. She didn't miss how buff he had gotten. He was under six feet, but his arms... He looked like he had taken up bench pressing as a new pastime, not that she had any idea what his pastimes were.

"Yup, going on five years now," Suzanne said. "So are you lost or something, or just slumming in Livingston?"

He didn't smile. There it was, that heavy gaze, those hazel eyes. He had a square face, a hard, chiseled look, and scars on his face from acne as a kid. To some, it was distracting. But there had always been something about Harold. He didn't fit the image of a typical pretty boy, didn't have the natural charisma, wasn't the total hot package that Toby was, but something about his personality and the way he moved gave him a level of attractiveness that kind of snuck up on her.

"Stopped in to visit my sister and her husband, who live here, after meeting with your brother today. Not slumming, just shopping on my way home," he said as if setting her straight, another reminder of the way he was.

She wasn't quite sure what to say to a man she had gone out of her way to avoid seeing for years even though she had known exactly where he was and what he was doing. She was rattled to hear that he had met with Marcus. Why hadn't her brother said anything? Then again, why would he?

"I see you're still with the Gallatin County sheriff's office," she said. "Still living in Bozeman?"

He said nothing but kept looking at her in that way of his, giving her everything, definitely not the self-centered, surface-level crap she'd become used to. She had to remind herself this was just a ruse. He was a player, too, and she'd never been able to wrap her head around how he'd yanked the rug right out from under her.

"I'm back in Gallatin, but maybe not for long."

"Back? Did you go somewhere?"

He hadn't looked away. It was unnerving, not something she was used to, considering Toby was always looking away. "Yeah, took a job down in Oklahoma City, with hate crimes. I've been back only a month."

So that was why she hadn't run into him. "Wow, I had no idea you were gone. So you're thinking of leaving again?" she said. What was it about hearing him now? She couldn't shake this unsettled feeling, considering how things had been left between them.

"Weighing options, is all," he said. There it was again, something in those hazel eyes—sadness or something else? She didn't know, considering she really didn't know him as she'd once thought she did.

"Well, this has been fun," she said, "but I've got a dinner date. I should be going. Great to see you."

She went to step away, but he pressed his hand to her

bare arm, glancing past her and then stepping in closer, really looking at her in a way that made her feel as if he were scrutinizing her, and she didn't have a clue why. For a second, she thought he was going to say something, but he stepped back and shook his head as if deciding not to. She hated when guys did that. Why did she have this feeling that so much between them had been left unsaid? Too much misunderstanding, betrayal, and uncleared air.

"What?" she said. Even she could hear how sharply it had come out.

"Nothing. Just…you look great, Suzanne. Hope life is treating you well. Stay safe out there," he said. Then he stepped around her and strode to the end of the aisle.

She took one last look at her basket, sure she had everything, and started to the cash register. She spotted him at the next till over, paying. The cashier laughed at something he said, and he took his plastic bag and turned to where Suzanne was paying for her own groceries. He just nodded at her as he walked on by. It was pure instinct to watch him. He was mysterious, sexy, and at one time, she'd thought he was the one.

"Is that everything?" the cashier said.

Suzanne had to pull her gaze away. "Yes, thank you," she replied, then tapped her debit card, took the groceries, and walked out of the store, into darkness.

She found herself looking around for a man that she shouldn't have been paying any attention. Because there was Toby, even if there was no commitment, no depth. What she did know was that tonight, she and Toby needed to have a talk or something to establish exactly which direction they were headed in.

Chapter 3

S he ran water in the sink, taking in her image in the mirror. The double sinks, walk-in shower and separate soaker bathtub, and even the matching towels were something she wouldn't have expected from a guy. Toby really had a nice place, with three bedrooms, two bathrooms, and an open layout, with light and windows.

Where was he now but in his kitchen, cooking pasta on the gas stove? Yet another feature she was trying to wrap her head around, considering all she'd done was hand him the groceries after he answered the front door of his spacious house at the edge of town.

She was still trying to settle her thoughts after running into a man she hadn't seen in years.

"Suzanne, dinner's up!" Toby shouted from across the house.

She turned off the water, dried her hands, and took in her image as she pulled the hair tie from her long dark hair, which she usually kept pulled back in a ponytail, and let it fall past her shoulders. She rang her fingers through it. She hadn't changed out of her dark uniform shirt, and she flicked the buttons one by one, seeing her practical sports bra underneath.

She stepped out into Toby's extremely neat and tidy master bedroom, with its queen-size light wood bed and furniture set, and tossed her shirt on his fashionable beige comforter, which matched everything else. If she didn't know better, she would've thought a woman had designed every part of this place.

She pulled open his chest of drawers, where she knew he kept his T-shirts, and lifted out a faded extra-large brown one to pull over her head before lifting her hair and striding out of the bedroom, down the hall to the kitchen, where Toby, who was dressed casually in blue jeans and a navy T-shirt, was draining the pasta into a large steel farmhouse sink.

He glanced over his shoulder as she stepped into his line of sight, and she wasn't sure what expression was on his face as his gaze lingered on her average-size breasts. "You helped yourself to my shirt?" he said.

For a second, she wondered if he had a problem with it. "I didn't change after my shift. Didn't think you would mind, or is it an issue?"

He pulled back and made a face. What that meant, she didn't know. "It's fine," he said, but she could hear the hesitation in his voice.

"Really? Because I'm getting the sense that maybe it isn't. I have to wonder what's going on with you, Toby."

He set the pot back on the stove, lifted the strainer from the sink, and dumped all the pasta into a big skillet of simmering sauce. He turned off the burner before resting both his hands on the counter and giving her everything in that one look, unamused. There was something about dancing around whatever this was. She didn't want to do it anymore.

"What is this, Suzanne? You've been off since you got here. I'm just making dinner for us, and then I want to chill after today. I have a lot on my mind and a lot of responsibility, too."

She couldn't shake the sense that he was keeping her at arm's length, and that was where he needed her to stay. She wasn't pushy, but she knew what she wanted.

"You know what, Toby? I'm not off, but I am wondering what this is. Can't remember ever feeling as I did tonight with my family. I was at my brother's place, texting you because I was expecting you to say where we should meet, and then I didn't hear from you for a few hours, so I was thinking, okay, maybe you were blowing me off. We had plans, I thought. So where were you?"

Had she always been this forward? Yes, when she needed to be.

She didn't pull her gaze from him as he stood there. It wasn't anything he said, but something about the way he was staring back at her gave her the feeling that maybe she shouldn't have asked.

He glanced away, and there it was, the difference between him and Harold. Maybe that was why she was so unsettled. Toby looked away far too often, she thought, when he should've been giving her everything.

"I have responsibilities, Suzanne. What is this?" Now he sounded defensive.

"So you were at the station? I left after you." She was sitting on one of the stools at the island, not pulling her gaze from him.

"I had a meeting with the chief."

She nodded. "So you were with the chief, then? Okay. The entire time?"

"Suzanne, why are you questioning me like this? I'm single, you're single. I don't answer to you, you don't answer to me." He gestured between them, and something about the energy left her feeling as if she had put her foot in her mouth. "I sense that you're upset about something. You had a bad day? It was a quiet day, though, so don't…"

Had he seriously just said that, a quiet day? She gave him a look, wondering what he was thinking, but he didn't seem to notice what he'd said. "Whoa, you know better than to say that," she snapped. "A quiet day…seriously, Toby?"

He seemed to shake her off. "A slip of the tongue is all, Suzanne. What I'm saying is you seem unsettled."

She hadn't expected this. "You know what, Toby? I guess I never really noticed it before, your unwillingness to answer me, how you so easily twist things, shining the situation back on me as if I'm the one with the issue. It's something politicians master, but then, maybe that's where you're heading."

Apparently, he got the zinger, as the laugh he let out was rough, jagged. "Wow, you really can be a piece of work sometimes."

She shrugged. "No, it's just that I asked you a question, and you deflected. You haven't really answered me. You're right that we're both single, but we're sleeping together, and I was under the impression that we were heading somewhere more serious. It didn't help that my brother and Charlotte both insinuated that you're playing me in some way. Are you playing me, Toby? Are you being straight with me? Come on, let's put our cards on the table and stop dancing around this."

"So now you're listening to your brother about me? Never thought that would be something you'd do, Suzanne. You think I care what Marcus thinks of me? I'm very well aware he doesn't like me and has no use for me. Just never expected that from you. Then there's Charlotte.

Everyone knows she always falls in line with how Marcus sees things."

Just the way he said it had her sitting up straighter.

"Are you trying to imply something about Charlotte?" She lifted her hand before he could reply. "No, don't, Toby, because that's low, even for you. Don't do that. Don't try to taint Charlotte's character to make yourself look good. She's a good woman, and you don't know her. Another thing is clear here, and maybe it's taken me really long to figure it out, but I get it now. You don't want to answer me. You have a way of deflecting that I never realized before. This thing here, Toby, what is it?" She gestured between them and didn't miss how uncomfortable he was. "I really want an answer. I think I deserve that much."

"Sounds to me like you're holding a gun to my head, Suzanne. A commitment, is that what you're looking for? Because we're not there. I like you, and you like me..." He just shook his head.

She wasn't a fool. She felt that sinking feeling in the pit of her stomach, sensing the brush-off that was coming, just as his cell phone started ringing. A second later, so did hers.

Of course, he didn't hesitate to answer. "Fire at the box store," he said. "We're being called in."

She reached for her phone, seeing the same message, and stood up, taking in the dinner they hadn't eaten. Toby was already walking to the door. She grabbed her purse before hurrying to his bedroom and grabbing her shirt, then to the front door, where he was waiting to lock up.

She was already halfway to her car when he called out, "Suzanne..." and she stopped, pulling the door open as he walked toward her.

"Look, I didn't mean to come down on you so hard or to sound like such a jerk," he said, "but at the same time, this here, between us, I don't know what to call it. I care about you. I really do…"

The way he was looking at her, the way he stepped toward her, the chemistry rocked, and she could feel the pull again, feel herself being reeled back into whatever this was.

"I sense a big 'but' coming."

He glanced away, hurried, brushing her off. He shook his head. "I like things the way they are. You just need to calm down a bit, not be so rushed. Besides, don't forget the little fact that I'm a lieutenant and you're not, and if others in the department get word of what's going on between us, things could become difficult, namely for me."

"Oh, I see. This is about your image, about protocol?"

He just shook his head and took a step back. "No, it's that everything isn't always that simple, Suzanne. Look, this isn't the time. We have a fire to get to, and I really want to talk to you about this when we're calmer, more reasonable, and have time."

He started over to his pickup, his new one, and she knew that was his way of shutting this down. There was just so much about Toby that she wasn't able to grasp. He had a way of not answering, of evading, of deflecting, and for the first time since this thing between them had started, she wondered if this was something he'd always done or if she was finally seeing this relationship for what it really was.

Would they ever settle into anything? Because right now, she didn't want to admit it, but there might be something to what her brother was saying. This could be going exactly nowhere.

Chapter 4

Returning to the same box store she'd left only an hour earlier, she found the parking lot was thankfully no longer full. Two firetrucks were on scene, and Toby was already geared up, heading toward the ladder truck that had just arrived with four volunteers who were waiting to receive orders.

Suzanne had on all her gear, her bulky turnout pants and jacket. She fastened it over Toby's shirt, which she was still wearing, as she started over to him, putting on her helmet and thick gloves. The smoke coming from the large building wasn't as heavy as she expected, but she was already assessing everything, making a plan, though she expected Toby to be on top of that. She was ready to shut down this fire before it grew into a blaze that would kill someone.

She spotted her brother with a few of his deputies and emergency personnel where the smoke was concentrated at the back of the store. A few people were hurrying out, wet from the sprinklers, which was good news. At least something was working in their favor.

"Do you think it's going to be a full-scale fire and we'll see some action?" said Everett, one of the senior volunteer firemen, who showed up at every fire. He hurried past her to stand before Toby, eagerly awaiting his orders, beat only by the newest volunteer firefighter, Greg. He was a full-time accountant, she thought, bored with life and looking for some excitement. Toby was engaged in a discussion with a man she assumed was in charge of the store.

"Not sure until we get in there," Suzanne said. "You know the thing about a fire: Smoke and flames can spread real fast. Any idea how it started or where?"

Near Toby, the volunteer firefighters were all vying for an exciting order that would have them in the thick of it. She just hoped she wouldn't be stuck babysitting them. Everett hadn't answered her.

The store manager was carrying on to Toby, likely having one of the worst days of his life. "It wasn't all that busy tonight," he said. "I don't know how many are in there, but as soon as I heard someone yell about smoke, fingers were pointing at who started it. We know it was that kid. It had to have been. He was up to no good when he walked in the store…"

She found herself looking around, willing Toby to get on with things and make sure everyone was out of the store, do a sweep, put out the fire, shut the power down, and avert disaster. There would be time after to figure out how it had started. Right now, he was still conversing and not ordering, and they were standing around with their thumbs up their asses.

Come on, Toby! The only orders were to get a team to assess the situation, another to perform search and rescue, and another to get the ladder truck up and onto the roof, where the smoke was. He had to get everyone where they needed to be.

"We're not sure if everyone's out yet, but deputies are inside, making sure," Toby said.

What the hell, Toby?

She couldn't believe he'd said that. Deputies weren't firefighters. What was he thinking? She was about to say something when he glanced her way.

"O'Connell, you're inside with Sweeney. The fire broke out in the change rooms at the back of the store. Sprinklers kicked in, but the water could do more damage to stock, so let's be mindful of what this could be costing the company, and be careful you're not doing more damage. We need this thing shut down quickly for the owner's sake." Toby was loud and commanding. He had that presence about him.

"What about doing a sweep of the store for any other civilians?" Suzanne said. "Why do you have deputies in there? Do we know how many are still inside, if there's still a fire or anyone trapped?"

She knew she was openly questioning him, but at the same time, she was the one who had walked him through these steps once, warning him about the changing conditions he should have been assessing from the moment he stepped on the scene. She'd been there to remind him before while teaching him in the field—fire behavior, fire suppression, and fire safety. Yet he was following none of it. Getting everyone out should've been his first priority, not preventing loss for the business.

For a second, she wondered where his head was. He'd said deputies were in there, but they were the last ones who should be doing that job. And protecting everything inside from any further damage…had he seriously said that? Yes, he had. She was already planning the talk she would have with him after this was over.

"Look, this place provides a lot of jobs, and we need

to make sure we keep it that way," Toby said. "Word already came down from the chief, so let's wrap this up quickly." He hadn't answered her, and he gave her only a distracted glance. Everything between them was all business.

Just as her brother Marcus made his way over, she shrugged on her air tank.

"We think almost everyone's out," Marcus said, "but I've still got a deputy inside, Harold Waters. He went back in after a woman said her sister was missing in the change rooms. We have no idea how many were in the store, though."

"Harold?" Suzanne said. "What is he doing there, and whose brilliant idea was it to send in deputies to get civilians out during a fire?"

Marcus was still walking beside her, gesturing to the store. He barely glanced her way. "Harold was first on scene, and I was second. Are we really having a pissing contest about who's doing what?" The way he said it had her shaking her head. Maybe he had some idea of her worries, as he continued: "Harold was out this way already. He's coming to work for me—just starting earlier than expected. That's right, you two know each other."

She knew Marcus wouldn't remember how close she and Harold had once been. So that was what Harold had meant about meeting with her brother. He was working there now.

"Fine, I get it," she said. "Now get your men the hell out of there. We're here, I'm here. Stick to what you guys do, arresting and keeping order. Keep the order out here so I can put the fire out in there. And do me a favor: Keep the rest of your deputies out. I don't need anyone else in there to rescue."

The front doors were wide open, and with the smoke

coming, she had no idea how many were still in the store. She didn't like this at all.

"I get it, Suzanne," Marcus said. "When you go in, send Harold out. I won't send anyone else, but at the same time, why hasn't Toby been all over this? His first priority should be getting everyone out, finding the fire, putting it out. You all are standing out here rather than getting inside and doing as you said, getting the people out."

What the hell was she supposed to say to that? He was right. She still couldn't believe Toby wasn't dragging the hoses in—screw the damage—just to make sure the damn fire was out. He needed to get the ladder truck up to the roof, where smoke was billowing, and cut through with an ax. That was what she'd have done, but then, she wasn't in charge.

She pulled in a breath, touching the top of her helmet. "What do we know about the fire, where it started? Anything I need to worry about inside?" It was something she should have heard from Toby, but he was likely still standing there, letting the manager ramble on.

"Suzanne, get in there!" Toby called out behind her.

Marcus glanced to him the same time she did as he walked her closer to the building. The visibility was low, and for a second, she wanted to set Toby straight. Like, what the hell was that?

"Just a lot of fuel for a fire, you know," Marcus said. "Most things in there, once a fire takes hold… It's not just food but clothing, houseware, furnishings. Everything will burn nicely if it takes off. Be careful."

At least Marcus stopped at the door. She took in people everywhere nearby and a deputy standing just inside without the needed equipment. Smoke inhalation could come out of nowhere. They were a small department with limited personnel, and something like this could suddenly become a five-alarm fire, with multiple lives at stake, and unlike stock, lives couldn't be replaced.

That was the call she'd expected, yet Toby seemed all about being a hero for the company. Carrying an ax in one hand, she glanced back to see Marcus moving people away just as Toby approached and touched her shoulder.

"Hey, Suzanne, let's do a quick sweep and make sure everyone's out. Then get these sprinklers shut off as soon as the fire's out. Let's be careful so I don't get my ass handed to me on a platter. Don't be so eager to put that through a wall or door if you don't have to," he said, gesturing to her ax.

Stuck on how tall, dark, and handsome he was, for a moment she felt as if he had her back. But at the same time, she wanted to remind him, lives first, property second. Hadn't she taught him that?

He shrugged on his tank, his mask around his neck like hers, helmet on, as they stepped into the store. Sweeney, she realized, was just ahead of them with an extinguisher. The grocery department on the right seemed not as affected.

"How long has this been going?" she said. "The clock is ticking."

Toby might be her boss, but it seemed she needed to remind him that smoke and toxic gas could spread in seconds. She heard someone calling out, past a display shelf, through the haze of smoke that continued through the store. The sprinklers were on. A man was on the ground, older, with a gash on his head. He had likely slipped and fallen on the slick floors.

"You take him out, and I'll do a sweep in back," she said to Toby, who was already helping the man up. She couldn't see anyone else.

"Suzanne, be careful, and remember what I said: Just

do the sweep, you and Sweeney. Contain that fire in back and get it out if it's not already."

Right, and what about the rest of the store? He should have ordered a coordinated search, done in grids, each of them taking a section, to make sure everyone was out. This was beyond a house fire, a barn, or anything he'd ever been in charge of. How was he not getting this?

She heard something, a shout, as she made her way through the haze, putting on her mask, as the smoke was getting thicker. She saw Sweeney with the extinguisher. It looked like the flames were out on a display of sweaters, and she tapped his shoulder.

"Get a hose back in here and soak this area," she said. "Is this where it started?"

Sweeney shook his head. "Smoldering is all I see. Not sure. The change rooms are over that way. Check it out while I finish here. There are just too many spots for something to take off."

She nodded and made her way over to the change rooms, hearing a voice again. Then she saw him, Harold, coming right toward her with a wet cloth pressed over his mouth and nose. She should've been angry, but her training kicked in, and she said, "Anyone back here?"

It took another second before she realized he hadn't known it was her, though he did by the time he gestured, pulled the cloth away from his face, and said, "Back office. Heard someone, but I can't get the door open." He took in her ax.

He didn't need to say another word. If the door wouldn't open and someone was in there, she'd use her ax without hesitation. And Toby? Well, he was just going to have to deal with it.

"Okay, I'll check it out," she said. "You need to get out of here."

All he did was shake his head and start moving toward the back of the store. "You got anyone else coming in?" he shouted.

There it was, the question she didn't want to answer. If she had been in charge, she'd have organized a grid search to account for everyone, but as far as she knew, it was just her and Sweeney, with Toby presumably still helping that old man out of the store.

"Just us," she said.

His eyes were questioning in response, but he turned and pulled her with him—and even though she was the firefighter, he moved her behind him.

Chapter 5

"**A**gain!" Harold said, then moved to take the ax from her, still holding the wet cloth over his nose. The smoke was thicker, and she couldn't hear anything else.

"No way! Seriously, Harold?" she yelled, gesturing for him to back up.

Just then, from beside them, another firefighter kicked in the heavy steel door, nearly splitting the frame she'd been trying to pry open with the ax and moving her aside. All of a sudden, he was there. She'd thought it was Sweeney, but she couldn't believe it was, in fact, Toby.

"Hey, what are you doing...?" she shouted.

The door crashed open. Inside the concrete room, a fan was running. They all moved inside, Harold already ahead. The man was on a mission, and she heard him yelling, looking around the room. The air seemed clear, not much smoke. It appeared to be a storage room, with a desk and metal shelves. A TV was on, and Harold pulled the plug on it as she heard the door close behind her. The only smoke in there had drifted in through the open door. It had been sealed well, which was both good and bad.

"Anyone in here?" Harold called out again.

Suzanne pulled off her mask and looked up at the low white ceiling. It was a box, contained. She glanced at the closed door behind them. It was time to go.

"Came to get you, is all," Toby said, pulling off his own mask. "I have that man out, with EMTs checking him over. Pretty sure no one else is in here."

The secure room at the back of the store was isolated. For a second, she didn't know what to say. Toby lifted his gaze to Harold, who was at the far end of the room, by the shelves. Everything was dry, no sprinklers, nothing on.

"No one's here," Harold said. His deputy shirt was covered in soot, and the wet cloth he was holding was likely a shirt he'd grabbed and soaked from the sprinklers. Smart, good thinking. "Must've been the TV I heard."

Toby was now on his radio.

Suzanne stepped over to Harold and rested the ax on the desk. "Well, then let's get out of here before the smoke is too thick. You aren't dressed for this, and you have no mask. You need to get yourself checked out by EMS, get some oxygen. You know the drill. What were you thinking, coming in here?"

He stepped over to her, closer. "I was doing my job, getting people out. You weren't here yet, but I was close by. Not sure what you're upset about, Suzanne. If it hadn't been for us, you would've found a mess here. You know, with smoke, people become disoriented quickly, and they were. In a huge store like this, not everyone had made it out. Now you're here, you can finish the job we started. There's no way to know who's still in here unless you have the numbers to search and make sure everyone's out. This is the worst situation. Everything about this works against you."

She noted the arrogance as he spoke. Those orders should have been coming from Toby. Being at a loss for words wasn't something Suzanne was known for. Harold gripped the shirt to his face and glanced past her, over to Toby.

"No one's here," he was saying. "It's clear in the back."

She thought she could hear Harris, another firefighter, replying with something about the fire not being contained to the building. It was coming from somewhere else.

"What?" Toby snapped. "What do you mean, it's not secure? Another fire, where?"

She didn't know where to look. She glanced back over to Toby just as Harold stepped closer to her.

"Okay, we're on our way out. Have Sweeney bring in the hoses, dammit. Wanted to avoid it. Get Greg and Everett to man the front of the store until other crews get here. I don't know if anyone else is in here."

She just stared at Toby, wondering what the hell he was doing. "What's going on?" she said.

Toby moved to the door, his mask back on. "More smoke is coming from the side of the building. One of the guys said there was a flare-up in sporting goods. They have propane tanks there, oil. We need to go…"

She could feel the situation spiraling into something that should never have been allowed. This could have been managed better, in an orderly and controlled way. Like, what the hell was Toby doing? He was completely blowing this. Crews and assignments were the first thing he should've handled.

"You need to make sure there's no one in here," Suzanne said. "You need to do a sweep of the store, section it off, send in teams and get the hoses in here to put this out. You should have done that already, Toby." She felt for a moment as if he were a probie she was having to give directions to.

He shook his head as if dismissing her. "You're not in charge here, Suzanne. I am. Now, let's go so I can fix this before it gets screwed up any more."

She was stunned at the amateurish move. He actually seemed to be blaming his fuck-up on everyone else. He pulled on the door, which seemed stuck. As Suzanne put her mask back, he was still having trouble with it.

"Shit…it's stuck," he said. He was pulling at the handle, his foot braced against the frame.

Harold stepped past her. He seemed to be putting it together, and she was positive he had already picked up on the fact that Toby had made a few bad calls.

"What the hell did you do to the door?" Harold snapped, now beside him. Both were trying to open it.

Suzanne reached for her radio and turned from the two of them. "This is O'Connell. We're trapped in an office at the left back of the store, not far from where Sweeney was last extinguishing a flare-up in clothing. The lieutenant is with me and Deputy Waters. I need you to send in someone to open it—"

She heard the boom. It felt as if something had exploded. The room shook, and she fell against the desk and glanced over to Harold, who was staring at the door. She already knew what had happened. Propane had exploded, and what should've been just a simple call, sweeping and finding people and dragging the hoses in to contain the fire, had turned into something completely dire.

All she could think as she reached for the ax was that there was no way in hell she was getting trapped in a burning building with both Harold and Toby all because of Toby's dumbass call.

"Move out of the way!" she said as she lifted the ax, but Harold grabbed the handle before she could take another step.

"Give me that ax," Toby said.

Suzanne just stared at the steel door, quickly catching on that smoke wasn't billowing in. She lowered the ax and shook her head.

"Nope," Harold said, then turned to Suzanne, though he had to know she wasn't the one in charge. "Right now, we're staying put until a hose is on that door. Your crews need to get back here and get us the hell out of the store. Whatever is on the other side right now, we need someone out there to assess it."

"We're sitting ducks in here," Toby started, and this time Harold turned to him, giving him everything.

"You're right, we are, but this room is sealed off from the rest of the store. Somehow, we're locked in here. With that explosion, who knows what'll happen when the door is opened? If it's all the same to you, get your people in here with a hose so they can clear the way, open the door, and get us out of here. If there's one thing I know about fires, it's that this explosion has turned something manageable into a shitstorm. You're in charge, but from where I'm sitting, you're screwing up, big time."

For a second, she wanted to back up Toby—but, though she didn't want to admit it, Harold was absolutely right.

Toby was pulling on the door again, and Harold was arguing with him. Between the two of them, this situation was ludicrous, so she took a step back and then another to really look at the room, leaving them to their male back and forth.

What made this really bad was seeing the reality of all the calls Toby was making. She'd never wanted to admit that Marcus could be right about Toby in any way. Had he always done this? It was hard to say, considering, since he'd been promoted over her, the only scenes he'd had to supervise were a backyard burn, an abandoned shed that had gone up in flames, and one housefire, where all he'd done was decide who would go in to put the fire out in the bedroom where it had started, who got to save the cat, and who got to go in and get the kids' shoes, because they were standing barefoot outside in the middle of the night. Good calls, but ones anyone could've made.

This situation was evidently one he wasn't able to navigate with the ease he should have.

"O'Connell, we're making our way back to you," said

Kyle, another of the full-time firefighters, who she was confident actually knew what the hell he was doing. "We have all hands on deck, though. Sporting department is engulfed. From what we can tell, they had a fresh shipment of disposable propane bottles and gas. They ignited, popping off like fireworks. We just learned of a paint supply, and then there's the ammo…"

She shut her eyes. This was just the worst of the worst cases, and here she was, stuck in the back, locked down, instead of helping. She knew her colleagues were now part of the rescue team.

"Okay, got it. Thanks for the update. Listen, in case I didn't say it, this room seems to be sealed off from the rest of the place, but if I'm hearing right and those bullets start going off…"

"Stay put," Kyle said. "Let us get this out, and then we'll get you. We've called in hazmat and another crew, because this is accelerating faster than expected. You have how much oxygen?"

Her tank still had about thirty minutes, but Harold had none. As he coughed, she could see smoke was now coming through the weakened door, and she knew they needed to hurry.

"You know what? Copy that, but smoke is now coming through the door. My tank has about thirty minutes, and Deputy Waters has no air tank, so whatever you're doing, you need to do it fast. Toby, how's your air holding up?" she said, knowing that Kyle would at least have every hose pointed their way to get them out.

He stopped and looked at his gauge. "Twenty-eight minutes."

"Harold, get away from the door," Suzanne said. "Here, put my mask on."

He put the cloth to his face again and strode over to

her, shaking his head as she went to take hers off. "No, you need it," he said.

Toby kicked the door. She could sense his frustration and the fact that he likely also wanted to kick his own ass. He'd made a lot of calls that could end badly for all of them.

"Let's see if we can block that smoke coming in," Suzanne said, gesturing around them. "This is a storage room. See if there's something we can use, blankets, anything."

Harold was already rummaging through the storage, the shelves, pulling things down. She didn't give Toby a passing glance as she followed, seeing boxes filled with what looked like patio cushions wrapped in plastic, and a box of shirts. Great, more stock that would be damaged.

"Here, give that here," Toby called out. When she threw it his way, he ripped open the plastic and stuffed the cushions around the door where smoke was coming in. She started rolling some of the shirts and handed them to him. The smoke was still there, but it wasn't coming in like it had been.

Toby rested his hand on the door, lifted up his mask, and walked over to where she and Harold were. Harold was leaning against the shelves, and she wasn't sure what to make of the way he was watching her and Toby. Did he have something to say?

"So let me get this straight," he said, then gestured to Toby. "You work for him?"

She knew he wasn't pulling any punches. It sounded accusatory.

"Yeah, that's right," Toby said. "I'm the lieutenant here, and Suzanne is one of my firefighters. Who exactly are you, Deputy? You shouldn't have been in here. Why the hell were you trying to get in here, anyway? You heard a TV?" He made a rude noise, giving attitude right back to him. "You're not a firefighter, and because of you, we're now trapped."

Suzanne couldn't believe him. She turned, really looking at Toby. Like, what the hell? This was the second time tonight he'd done that, blaming others.

He groaned and sighed, then lifted his hand. Maybe it was the expression on her face that had him dialing it back and saying, "Sorry, that was uncalled for."

"We're not getting into a finger-pointing contest here," she said. "It doesn't matter who did what and who's to blame. Harold thought he heard someone in here. You'd have done the same, and so would I. There's no way any of us could've known it wasn't a real person in here, so knock it off. The only thing that matters is getting out. So you and you, just knock it off. If we really want to settle things, Toby, you should've had everyone in here, making sure this place was searched for shoppers, getting the hoses dragged in and everything put out. Since we're at it, how about telling me what that was about, worrying about keeping damage as minor as possible? Sounds to me like you were more interested in protecting this property than saving lives. It was a bad call, Toby, and you know it."

She always knew when Toby had been pushed too far. There was just something about him, a point where he stopped listening.

"It sounds like you're questioning my authority, Suzanne," he said. "You sure this isn't because of tonight and you being pissed at me?"

She could feel Harold watching and knew he was taking in all of this and more. He wasn't stupid, but she had to remind herself he was dishonest.

"Don't flatter yourself, Toby," she said. "You think I can't separate our personal lives from the firehall? I can.

Our relationship outside of here has nothing to do with me calling you out on your bad decisions. You're in way over your head, Toby, and us being in here is all on you. I trained you and taught you better than this. You need to assess the situation and protect lives first. You should be out there, leading, yet you're in here. You're not up to this task, and you're choking."

She knew she was crossing a line, but at this point, he was really screwing up big time. Any good leader knew when to ask for help and admit wrongdoing, but then, come to think of it, she couldn't remember a time when Toby had ever accepted he was fallible.

"Well, maybe I'm here to watch your ass, Suzanne! You ever think of that? Look, you know I care…" He stopped and made a rude noise.

She could feel Harold giving everything to them.

"So you two are, what, dating, married, together…?" Harold gestured between them.

She stayed silent at first, considering that question was a source of contention between them. "We're nothing," she said, looking right at Toby. "Right? As you said, let's not put a label on it or get too serious."

For a second, she thought he'd snarl. "Look, this isn't the time for this discussion," he said, then walked over to the door and kicked it again.

She wanted to call out to him that kicking doors wasn't going to solve anything, but she didn't.

Harold was looking at her in a way that was really uncomfortable. "Is he always like this?" he said.

She gave everything to him. "He's doing his best, Harold. It doesn't help, having everyone coming at him."

"Is that what you think this is?"

She leaned against the shelves, wondering how long it would take to get them out of there. This was becoming personal and uncomfortable, and neither of the men had any place in this situation. "I don't know, Harold. What is this? I haven't seen you in years, and then here you are. Why did you take the job working for my brother?" She wasn't sure what to make of his expression, the way he was looking at her.

"Why would you care who I work for? It's not as if we're together, Suzanne. If I recall, you broke up with me, but I'm sensing it bothers you, and I guess I don't understand why."

How could he not get it?

"There's history between the two of you?" Toby said. She hadn't even realized he was standing there, listening.

"Well, it seems I'm trapped in a storage room with two men I've slept with. Yes, Toby, Harold and I were involved once. We dated as seniors in high school. He was my high school sweetheart, my first love—and then he broke my heart."

Harold narrowed his eyes, furrowed his brow. She could see something, confusion, disbelief, and she made herself look away and give everything to Toby. He said nothing, but she didn't miss how curious he seemed. If the situation weren't so dire, she thought this moment could've been comical. Maybe she'd look back on it in a few decades and be able to laugh.

"Well, I guess I'm at a loss," Harold said. "You say I broke your heart, but that's not how I remember it."

She couldn't believe he could be that arrogant. "Wow, amazing. You sleep with my best friend and you don't think I would be hurt? You're a piece of work, Harold."

For a second, from the expression on his face, it seemed he didn't remember what he'd done.

"Slept with your best friend?" he said. His voice was deep, and his eyes simmered with passion, a kind of anger she didn't remember. He took a step closer to her. "That's absolute bullshit, Suzanne. Let's set the record straight. One minute, we were together, and the next, you were telling me we were over and you'd suddenly made plans to go to the prom with Wes Parker. That's what I remember. So you want to talk about who gutted who? No, better yet, let's not."

Chapter 7

W as he serious? Evidently so.

She took in the room. More smoke was coming in, and after Harold started coughing again, she pulled off her mask and pressed it to him, making him breathe in the air.

Toby now had his mask on. "Suzanne, put your own mask on and stop playing hero," he yelled at her.

She just shook her head, but Harold pushed it away. She pressed it to her face and breathed in the air, keeping Harold right there so she could pass it back to him.

He seemed furious, and she was still stuck on the fact that he didn't remember that Saturday night with Jessa Armstrong. It was so long ago, but it felt like just yesterday. Toby was watching her and Harold, and she wasn't sure what was there in his expression. Fighting this fire was the only thing that should be their focus, not a school love affair gone bad.

"So tell me about this best friend I supposedly cheated on you with," Harold said. "I'm dying to hear this,

Suzanne. Always wondered why you did what you did, yanking the rug right out from under me."

He was standing so close, but she was well aware that Toby was only a few feet away. Talk about a love triangle gone wrong. This wasn't something she wanted to discuss, let alone have Toby hear it.

"You want to talk about Jessa, really? Because I don't. It may have been a long time ago, but having a reminder of the fact that you slept with my best friend and couldn't even be honest that it happened? I never expected that from you, Harold. That just shows how little I knew you. I cursed you and hoped every bad thing happened to you because of what you did to me."

His jaw slackened as if he had something to say, and she could see the frustration. She'd expected shame or embarrassment at the reminder that he'd been a dirty dog, but all she saw was the opposite.

"That's absolute bullshit! However you came up with that story, it never happened. You really think I would do something like that to you?" He made a rude noise and then coughed again.

She pulled off her mask and put it over his face, making him take in the air, breathe it in. "You say that's bullshit, so even all these years later, you don't want to come clean?"

He pushed the mask away and actually forced it back over her face, making her breathe. "Who told you I slept with Jessa? Let me guess…it was Jessa herself?"

For a second, she didn't know what to say. She had believed something for so long, but now, as she stood there, she didn't know what to think.

He was shaking his head and was so close to her, holding the mask to her face. "And you believed her. You think I would do that to you, to us?" He shook his head, sounding so accusatory. "Who's the asshole now, Suzanne? No, I never slept with her—"

"But you took her to prom," she said, cutting him off.

He coughed again. Everything about this situation was dire. "I took her to prom because you ended us just like that, and you were with some other guy. I did it to hurt you, but how do you think I felt, watching you just laugh and have fun and party with some other guy, his hands all over you? And you let him, after all we'd been through together. You made everything about us seem like a lie. So when she asked me, damn right I said yes. But you know what really gets me, Suzanne, is the fact that you so easily believed it. What does that say about us?"

He started coughing again, and she managed to get her mask off her face and put it on him. She couldn't figure out how to handle what he was saying. This was crazy. Why wouldn't he just admit what he'd done? It didn't matter now. She was so over him. Right?

"Are you telling me my best friend lied to me? Why would she do that? That's crazy. She was my best friend…"

He was breathing in the air, and she lifted her jacket over her mouth, her nose, as she leaned there against him. He must have known she was struggling as she coughed, as he pulled the mask away.

"Put this damn thing on and keep it on," he said. "You know, what I don't get, Suzanne, is how you could believe a lie so easily. She told you we slept together, and instead of coming to me, you automatically believed her?" He was holding the mask to her face so tight. He was so close. "You know Jessa always wanted me. She'd hit on me more than a few times while we were together, but I told her no. Yet the minute she ran to you and said that I slept with her, you believed her, you cut both of us off, and it was that

47

easy for you. No, let me guess, you were still friends with her…?" He shook his head.

She was still at a loss for words, because that was exactly what she'd done. She'd believed her best friend over a guy she was totally, madly in love with. She couldn't have been that stupid. "You're wrong about it being easy on me. It wasn't easy. It gutted me that you could cast me away that easily, as if I was nothing. Just tell me the truth. It doesn't matter now, not anymore. When I saw you take her to prom…"

"You, what, assumed it was true?" He coughed again, and she took in Toby standing there, hearing all of it. "You're wrong, Suzanne. It does matter. It matters to me, because it says everything of who I am, of who you are, of who we are. You're right, though. It wasn't easy…"

"We're not talking about Jessa Armstrong, city councillor, running for mayor?" Toby said, cutting in.

Suzanne rested her hand on Harold's arm, taking in Toby, a man she had slept with and was pretty sure she loved. There he was, listening to her talking to another guy about their relationship, their mistakes.

"The very same," she said.

Harold had started coughing again but was still holding the mask to her face. Everything about him showed her the man he was, and it erased everything she had believed for so long. He should hate her, but he was doing everything he could to protect her.

When he slid to the floor, she heard the crash of the door and knew help had arrived.

Chapter 8

Lights were flashing, engines were running, and hoses were being dragged out into the parking lot so that Greg, one of the volunteers, could roll them up. The parking lot was flooded, but the fire was out now for the most part, thanks to Kyle, who'd turned on the force of the hoses and soaked everything. The sporting, clothing, and outdoor departments were completely destroyed, and smoke and water damage had likely ruined the rest of the store. Suzanne distantly heard the yelling between firefighters and the police who controlled the scene and kept everyone back.

Harold was sitting on the back bumper of an ambulance with an oxygen mask on. Roxy, the EMT on that night, had dark hair, big eyes, and full hips, and Suzanne could see that Harold was giving her a hard time. Suzanne strode over to the back of the ambulance. Now was time for the cleanup, and she needed a minute to come to grips with what had almost happened. Marcus was lingering there, too, leaning against the side of the ambulance, his foot resting on the bumper, saying something to Harold.

"Look, I'm fine," Harold said. "I'm not going to the hospital. There are other people here who need your help…"

"And you're one of them," Marcus said, intervening, then turned to Roxy. "How's he doing? Harold, the only thing that's going to come out of your mouth next is that yes, you're going to the hospital, even if I have to tie you to the gurney. I watched you get dragged out of there. You passed out and breathed in too much smoke."

Suzanne was aware how stubborn Harold could be.

Roxy was taking his blood pressure. "His oxygen levels are low," she said. "It would be best if he went to the hospital, but he keeps insisting he's not going."

Harold pulled the mask away from his face again. He was pale, but she could see he was getting ready to argue.

"Put it back on," Roxy ordered and grabbed the mask, pressing it to his face, holding it there.

When Suzanne stepped up to the ambulance, every-one's eyes were on her. Marcus's gaze was heavy, question-ing. He likely wanted to have a word with her.

She pulled at the Velcro of her jacket and opened it. "Harold, you collapsed. You breathed in a lot of smoke. Go to the hospital and get checked out. It took two of the firefighters to carry you out of there."

"If I recall, you breathed in about as much smoke as I did," Harold said, pulling his mask away again. "Have you checked Suzanne out yet?" He dragged his gaze from her over to Roxy and made a point of including her brother, who hadn't pulled his gaze from her since the moment she'd walked over.

The strap from her helmet was hanging loose, and she was gritty and wanted a long, hot, steamy shower. She real-ized she hadn't said two words to Toby since they'd been pulled from that back room. Where was he now? Right back in charge as if he were responsible for saving everyone's asses and putting out this fire. Everything about this situation left her feeling unsettled.

"He's right, Suzanne," Roxy said. "Humor me and sit down. You know better." She gestured to a spot beside Harold, and Marcus actually reached over and took her helmet from her head.

"Yup, come on, Suzanne, sit," he said. "Let Roxy check you over, run another oxygen mask…"

"If I needed oxygen, I'd be the first over here, asking for it. You know that, Roxy…" she managed to get out, but as soon as she sat, her legs wanted to give out. Weariness, likely. She was shaken in a way she'd never experienced before, but then, she'd never been trapped like that. It bothered her now in ways she knew weren't rational. She didn't have to look over to Harold to know he was watching her. She could feel his warmth. Her adrenaline was still pumping.

"Then you won't mind sitting for a bit," Roxy said. "Come on, Suzanne, jacket off. You know the drill."

There was something odd about sitting side by side with Harold, who was holding an oxygen mask to his face. Marcus was standing there, taking in everything.

"So what happened in there, Suzanne?" he finally asked as Roxy pumped up her blood pressure cuff, which pinched.

"Hey, careful," Suzanne snapped.

Roxy just shook her head as if she were overreacting as she reached past her for an oxygen mask and actually set it over her nose and stretched the elastic around her head to hold it on. She was reluctant to say it, but she could feel how much even the first pull of oxygen helped, how much she needed it.

"It was as I told you, Marcus," Harold said. "I thought

I heard someone, but it was just a TV. We got trapped. The door wouldn't open, and, well, you know the rest. We're out. They didn't find anyone else in there, did they?"

The way Harold had jumped in, leaving out all of Toby's dumbass moves, she wondered why he'd do that. At the same time, she was still reeling over what he'd said earlier. Had Jessa really lied, and she'd believed her that easily? It was something she needed a moment or even a good night's sleep to consider and think on.

She pulled the mask away from her face. "It was a little more than that, Harold," she said. "I know Kyle made sure they went through the place after the fire was out. Everyone got out."

No thanks to Toby, she thought, but she was sure he'd learned a lesson from this. She knew he was upset, but it could've been so much worse. He'd yet to say anything to her. It was awkward, unsettling.

"We're fine, Marcus," she finished. "Everyone is."

Roxy ripped the blood pressure cuff off her. "Okay, just sit there with that mask on until I tell you to get up."

"She good?" Marcus asked. Suzanne wondered if he was going to insist she go to the hospital, too.

"Yeah, she'll be okay. She should get checked out at the hospital, though. You know the dangers of smoke inhalation, Suzanne—the dangers to the heart and respiratory system. Don't play the hero here."

She was about to argue when Marcus said, "She won't, because she's going to the hospital along with my deputy. I'll wrap up things here. Harold, no more arguing, and you're not to leave the hospital until the doctor looks you over and gives the okay." He put his booted foot on the ground.

Suzanne spotted Toby coming their way.

"She okay there, Roxy?" he called out from a few feet

away. He'd given her only a passing glance. What that was about, she didn't know.

"She's going to the hospital with the deputy to get checked out," Roxy replied.

Marcus hadn't pulled his gaze from him, and he was starting to walk his way. She went to pull her mask off when she felt a hand on her arm. Harold, who gestured with his chin for her to stay. Maybe he knew what she was thinking, what she was going to do. She was about to stand up.

"No, stay out of it." He was so direct.

"Stay out of what?" She knew she sounded defensive.

His face was so close. His hazel eyes held a confidence she'd not seen before. "It's your brother's right to speak to him. He's got some things to say, so let him."

"He's shoving his nose in my business," she snapped. She took in Toby, who was now just a ways off from the ambulance, his helmet still on, the strap loose and hanging. Marcus was right in front of him. Whatever he was saying, she couldn't make it out.

"Yeah, well, he's got a right to be upset," Harold said. "So you're really involved with him?"

Roxy was listening, she knew. She wondered if Harold had picked up on the fact that she and Toby hadn't officially shared their non-dating status with anyone at the station.

She said nothing, just took in Toby's face. The expression there wasn't happy. He stepped around her brother and started over to her. He allowed his gaze to fall to her as he stopped right in front of her.

"You okay?" was all he asked.

She nodded and went to pull the oxygen mask away, but he pulled off his gloves, reached over, and pressed the mask back to her.

"No, leave it on," he said. "Listen, I know we need to talk, and we will. You and the deputy will go to the hospital. I have to finish up here."

For a second, she thought he was going to say something else.

He slid his gaze over to Harold, then took a step back and said to Suzanne, "After I wrap up everything here, I'll come by and get you." He turned away. "Roxy, make sure she goes to the hospital and gets checked out, and the deputy too."

It was exactly the conversation she hadn't expected.

Harold stood up, pulled his oxygen mask off, and held out his hand to her. "Come on, Suzanne," he said. "Get in."

Chapter 9

Her doorbell was ringing.

Her head throbbed as she opened her eyes, blinking in the light that spilled into her bedroom. She ran her hand over her face. Her long hair was a tangled mess, and she brushed it back from her face and out of her eyes as she put her feet on the floor, climbing out of her double bed. Her small bedroom had a dresser, a night stand, and a tiny closet, but instead of looking through it for clothes to put on, she stayed in her pajama shorts and T-shirt.

The floor creaked. She didn't bother looking through the peephole before she pulled open the door. There was Toby, two coffees in hand, appearing freshly showered, with a smile on his face.

She hadn't expected that. At the same time, she felt as if she could use another hour or two of sleep and a couple of Tylenol to clear the achy cobwebs in her head.

"You're here awfully early," she said. "You brought me coffee... What time is it, anyway?"

Toby stepped inside, and Suzanne stepped back after

taking the coffee from him. "You're welcome, by the way—and it's not that early. It's after ten," he added teasingly.

She lifted the lid of the takeout coffee and took a swallow, unsure what to make of this.

"How'd you sleep?" he said. For a moment, it sounded like concern.

She turned and strode the few steps to the tiny kitchen of her one-bedroom house. She rested the coffee on the counter and opened the cupboard beside the sink for a bottle of Tylenol and a glass.

"Oh, you know, pretty good, I guess," she said.

Actually, she'd slept like shit, considering it had been close to three in the morning by the time she'd arrived home after Toby picked her up from the hospital, something else she hadn't expected. She opened the bottle and tapped two pills into her hand, then filled a glass of water and swallowed them both down, feeling the rawness in her chest from the smoke.

"Liar," he said. "Seriously, Suzanne, I should have stayed last night. I was worried. I shouldn't have left you alone. You have no idea how worried I was."

What was it about the way he was looking at her that had her wanting to wrap her arms around herself? It was a feeling of discomfort she hadn't felt in a while. She downed the rest of the water and filled another glass from the tap, then swallowed some more.

"You left because I told you to go," she said. "You think I would've let you stay because you insisted? As you said to me last night before the fire, and let me remind you of it, you want to keep it simple, not too serious. You know we don't stay over at each other's places. We're not there yet, or rather, you don't want to be there yet. Hell, you can't stand to be seen with me in public."

Okay, so she was still pissed over everything, not just

about Toby but also about Harold, about learning that something she'd believed with everything in her heart wasn't true.

He said nothing, but he was still standing there. Good God…he was so good looking. His blue eyes gave everything to her before he glanced away, just something he did.

"Maybe I've changed my mind," he said. "It was too close last night, Suzanne, and maybe that was a wakeup call for me. I told you I care, but maybe I care more than I want to admit."

There it was, something she'd have given anything to hear. But right now she wasn't sure how she felt about anything, considering he couldn't even hold her gaze as he said it. Deep and personal was something Toby wasn't.

Then there was Harold. Damn him! She hadn't thought of him in a long time, and now she couldn't get him out of her mind.

"You know, when the call came in last night, we were in the middle of settling a few things," she said. "You never answered me about where you were, and I didn't push, but I'm pushing now. You were over two hours late, and when you didn't hear from me after you finally texted, you said you were just about to go out. Then in the next breath, you said you wanted to stay in. Yeah, Marcus and Charlotte got in my head about you and said some things that pissed me off, but at the same time, Toby, you never really answered me about where you were and who you were with."

He groaned and lifted his gaze to the ceiling as if she were creating a problem, something else he did that she didn't like. "Seriously, Suzanne, are we going back to that? Fine, I had a meeting, which I told you about. Besides, I had news to share, though you didn't give me a chance. "It seems I'm in line for another promotion to captain. It should be coming down any day. Wanted you to be the first to know. At the same time, it kind of complicates things for us."

She just stared at him, realizing he was serious. "You're being promoted to captain?" She was positive her voice squeaked. Her head was pounding, and she was having trouble understanding what he'd said. He was smiling at her over news that she shouldn't have been hearing. "I don't understand," she finally said, then reached for the coffee and took a swallow, hoping the caffeine would bring clarity to the situation.

He'd screwed up so badly the night before that anyone else would've been better qualified for that promotion. This really was an absolute gong show.

He let out a rough laugh. She could see she was stepping on his very male alpha ego, and she realized he'd been expecting her to be all happy and make a fuss over him. That was exactly what she'd done when he'd made lieutenant over her, but not this time.

"Well, we've kept this between us, on the down low, but we're going to have to make it more formal and disclose to everyone with my upcoming promotion, as it would be frowned on. There would be accusations of favoritism, you know, from the other firefighters, thinking you're getting special attention, better assignments at fires and everything, because we're involved, so we'd have to…"

"Just dial it back a second. Are you expecting me to take a back seat on fire calls because we're involved? Let's be clear on exactly what you're saying here." She knew she sounded pissed, but at least her head wasn't throbbing like it had been seconds ago. It was likely the water and the Tylenol that had eased the ache.

"Well, I don't want to seem like I'm favoring you, so I'll have to be sure I'm giving assignments to everyone, not just you. I know you're good, but at the same time, Suzanne, it could be tricky..." He was so matter of fact, and that wasn't even the most absurd part of this, as she realized he was serious.

"Wait, stop talking. Let me get this straight. You're being promoted by who?" She held the coffee in front of her, feeling so grungy and wanting a shower, furious over what she was hearing.

His smile faltered. "Well, Chief Burns, of course," he said.

She knew her jaw slackened. She pictured the chief, who'd never given her a passing glance. He was a man steeped in the community, with deep roots, and she wondered how much of this was as Marcus had said.

"Not your grandfather?" she said.

He stepped back as if she'd slapped him. The smile he'd had before was suddenly gone. "What does my grandfather have to do with this, with my promotion?"

If it had been any other time, she likely wouldn't have pushed, not with Toby, not with how she felt about him, but at the same time, after the night before, and considering her experience and qualifications, she was realizing the only qualification Toby had was the fact that his grandfather had handpicked Chief Burns for the job, and he still very much had his hand in the running of things from his retirement, which he spent fishing and seeing to it that his grandson would soon be the next chief. Why hadn't she seen it before?

She shook her head and rested her coffee back on the counter. "He has everything to do with this, Toby. Did you ever ask yourself why you got the promotion to lieutenant when you hadn't been with the department that long? I trained you, yet I wasn't even considered. I have more experience, and so does Kyle. If it weren't for him, things last night could have gone a lot worse. You didn't handle that call well, and I'm not sure why you didn't send in everyone right from the get-go to do a sweep of the store and drag the hoses in. You were more worried about keeping the damage to a minimum when there was a fire that could've killed people. Then us getting trapped back there after you closed the door, when we ended up locked in…"

"We wouldn't have been back there if it weren't for that old boyfriend of yours!" he snapped. "A TV, seriously? It sounds to me as if you're trying to saying this is sexist in some way. You think you were more deserving of the promotion to lieutenant?" He actually took a step closer to her, and for a second, she had to remind herself this was Toby, and she really liked him, but right now, she was positive he couldn't see it, or maybe he didn't want to see it.

"I trained you to go into a fire and look at everything, to rescue people and contain the fire and get it put out, but last night you acted like a rookie, Toby—and I'm not saying this to hurt you, but promotion to captain…?" She shook her head and took in the flicker in his blue eyes. It was the kind of anger that simmered. She'd never seen him like this.

He leaned in. "Rookie? I'm no rookie, but let's talk about who did what. Just what the hell were you thinking, taking off your mask? You put yourself in danger, and that's not something you do. The deputy shouldn't have been back there. I came to get you. The fact that you're insinuating in some way that I'm not qualified…" He shook his head and stepped back, and she had the sinking feeling that she'd just made things worse. Angry Toby was who was standing there with her. "No, if anything, your dumbass move could've cost you your life. I should write you up, and if you were anyone else, I'd be forced to, but right now, I'm playing favorites."

She was stunned over what he'd said. It was ridiculous, but at the same time, she realized he could write her up for anything now, and what could she do about it?

He lifted his hands and started walking away. "Take the rest of the week off, Suzanne. Don't come back to work until you have an okay from the doctor." Then he was at the door, his hand on the door handle, still holding the other coffee. He seemed to hesitate a second. "I'm sorry you feel this way and can't be happy for me, but there's more to consider when you're in charge. The fire last night cost the community hundreds of jobs. Being in charge isn't just about the easy choices. You have to make the tough choices, too. Sorry you can't see that." He pulled open the door and glanced back to her. "And for the record, yeah, I was out with someone—but it's not what you think."

Then he stepped out of her house and closed the door, and she just stared at it, feeling the bite of his words, wondering where exactly their relationship stood.

Chapter 10

There was something about how things had been left with Toby. Suzanne couldn't shake the feeling that she'd jammed her foot in her mouth in a way she didn't know how to fix. At the same time, she didn't think she'd made her point clearly. If it had been anyone else promoted over her, she didn't think it would have bothered her so much, but she really cared about Toby, and she didn't know how she was supposed to continue down this line, where it was becoming clear she would have to downplay her skill and put herself second.

It was something Marcus had said to her: "Don't be that girl." And that was never the kind of girl she had been —until she met Toby.

She jammed her hand over her forehead as she sat behind the wheel of her car, feeling as if the world were showing her a side of itself that she'd never seen before.

Then there was Harold, who'd continued to be someone else entirely. After hating him and being angry at him for so long, she was at a loss for what to do, feeling so many things, confusion being one of them. She took in

City Hall and stepped out. Her phone was ringing, and saw it was her mom.

"Hey, Mom," she said as she closed her car door, lifting the purse she rarely carried over her shoulder. She was dressed casually in a light blue T-shirt and blue jeans, her hair hanging loose, and she took in the people striding by. She didn't look right at anyone but gave the phone all her attention.

"Are you okay? Heard about the fire, and Marcus told me you were at the hospital last night. You should have called! The news said it was bad, that two firefighters were trapped and they didn't know if they'd get them out. I called Marcus when I didn't hear from you, Suzanne. He told me it was you."

That was one thing about Marcus: He shared just about everything with their mom when it came to one of them being in trouble. At the same time, he somehow avoided sharing anything about what he did, as he didn't cross that line when it came to his own duties as a cop.

"It was nothing," she said. "A fire at the mall. You know how the news blows everything way out of proportion. I breathed in a little smoke, no big deal. I'm fine and taking a few days off."

"Well, that's good, then, but you've always let me know you're okay with a text or phone call after a big night, especially something serious. You didn't this time."

She shut her eyes and wanted to kick herself, because she'd totally forgotten, what with everything that had happened. Considering everything that had gone down the night before, calling her mom had been the furthest thing from her mind.

"Sorry, Mom, it was just one of those things. But I assure you I'm fine. The fire's out, and it was just a back room we were stuck in, not even for that long. We were out in no time. It wasn't even that big of a deal. The hospital was only a precaution, an overreaction, really. No big deal…" She wondered if her nose had grown, because her mom said nothing on the other end for another second. How much detail had Marcus given her?

"You can come by later today, then," she said. "I have Eva, and Alison is on her way over. We're baking. Luke has been shipped back to God knows where, Owen is out of town, Karen and Jack are working on some big case, and Ryan and Jenny are taking off for a few nights. Since you have time off, why don't you come by, as well? The girls would love it, and you can show me you're okay. Heard from Marcus that he's hired Harold Waters as one of his lead deputies, too. You remember Harold, don't you? I think you two dated in high school…"

Her mom was still going on, and she wanted to kick Marcus. Just then, she spotted Jessa walking out of City Hall, her short dark hair perfectly groomed, looking curvy in a light pantsuit and heels, exactly whom she wanted to have a minute with.

"You know what, Mom? I've got to go. There's someone I'm meeting with. Listen, I'll come by later." Then she hung up, tucked her phone in her purse, and started walking toward Jessa, who she noticed was waving at someone.

She looked over and spotted Harold, wearing his deputy uniform, hat, and shades. He too was walking toward Jessa, and what did she do but stand there like a fool, watching as if he were a train racing off the tracks? She fisted her hands and took another step.

Jessa gave a swoopy wave with that over-the-top smile that everyone loved, wearing her perfect makeup and big sunglasses. "Harold Waters, why, I couldn't believe it when

I heard you're joining the sheriff's department here!" she called out.

Suzanne wasn't sure if he smiled, but she felt like an absolute fool, standing there, feeling the same ache she'd felt so many years ago because of the actions of a man she'd loved like a fool and a best friend she'd shared all her secrets with. She made herself take a step closer, not hearing what Harold said. Jessa actually pulled him into a hug, and she noticed his reluctance as he stepped back. The tightness in her stomach had her moving closer, walking right toward them, really digging into each step. Then they were both looking her way.

"Oh, Suzanne… Hey there, girl! What a surprise this is, both you and Harold. You remember Harold Waters?"

She couldn't believe Jessa had said that to her, and maybe it was the look she gave her that made Jessa quickly continue.

"I heard about the fire last night," she said. "Are you okay? Was just telling all this handsomeness about how happy we all are he's joined the department. I know I'll sleep so much better knowing he's here, watching over all of us. Oh, that's right!" She actually gasped. "You two were in the fire last night, trapped. Wasn't that hottie lieutenant with you, as well?"

Right, so there was already talk, of course. Jessa had always been a flirt with Toby, too, even though she was married to a man Suzanne had met a time or two, Robert Blyth, a computer technician who shared her same big personality.

"You're okay, both of you? Oh my goodness, it's been all over the council. What an awful thing that was, what happened. I heard they have a suspect already for the fire, that it was arson. It's just horrible that such a thing can happen here in our community. Why, I hope they throw the book at him. All those people who have lost their jobs, it hurts, really hurts us…"

Jessa could go on and on, but Suzanne was stuck on the mention of a suspect, considering she was way out of the loop.

Harold had stayed silent so far. "You know we can't comment on the investigation," he finally said.

Suzanne crossed her arms and took in Jessa, still struggling with what she'd learned from Harold. She wondered how many more people from Livingston would stop her and comment on the fire and the fact that she'd been trapped. She wanted to know who it was they suspected.

"You okay?" Harold asked, giving everything to her, only she couldn't see his hazel eyes behind his shades.

She didn't feel like discussing any of what had happened in that fire with Jessa standing there, and she wasn't sure what to make of the way she was watching the two of them. "Yeah, good," she said. "I didn't see you at the hospital before I left. You back to work today?"

Jessa, who was at least three inches shorter than her, was looking up from her to Harold. What she was thinking, Suzanne didn't have a clue. She was still working on the words to ask her why she'd lied.

"I am," he said. "I take it you're off today?" He took in her casual attire.

What was she supposed to say, that her boss had ordered her off because he was angry—no, furious with her? "I am. Was just on my way over to see you, Jessa. I wanted to have a word with you."

Harold slid down his shades and peered over them to her. Of course, he knew what she was doing, even if Jessa didn't.

"You were coming to see me?" Jessa pressed her hand to her chest, sounding truly shocked. Their friendship had fizzled out into an acquaintance. At social functions, they'd still talk, but sharing deep secrets was something they no longer did.

"Yeah, I was. I wanted to talk to you about some things."

Harold didn't pull his gaze from her, still giving everything to her, and she wasn't sure what to make of that.

"Well, I'm just on my way to a council meeting, and then I have to pick up Leanne at preschool—my daughter," she added to Harold, including him in the conversation. "I'm married now, two kids." She sang out the last part and held up her hand, showing the big rock. Then she ran her hand over Harold's arm. "Why don't you come by tomorrow, and we can talk then, Suzanne? Maybe we should do lunch. We could catch up, or maybe a girls' night out? It's been a long time. Harold, you too. I'll have you over for dinner sometime, and you can meet my family."

That was just something about Jessa: She could go on and on.

"You know what, Jessa?" Harold said. "I want to have a word with Suzanne. It was good to see you."

"Oh, you too, Harold," Jessa said. "Suzanne, listen. Call my office and talk to Barbie, and ask her to put you on the schedule tomorrow. We'll catch up." Then she lifted her hand, and her cell phone started ringing from inside the purse that dangled from her arm. She answered it and walked away, leaving Suzanne standing there with Harold.

It was just her and him, and the anger she'd felt for so long now had changed into something that confused the hell out of her.

Chapter 11

"What are you doing?" Harold said. He was standing right in front of her, and she took in his face, the scars that she really had to look to see. There was something about the way he stood, the way he gave everything to her; she found herself comparing him and Toby, two very different men with two very different personalities.

He had tucked his shades into his shirtfront now. His hazel eyes were so distinct, and his arms and chest were so damn impressive. She had to fight the urge not to stare as he took another step toward her. One more and she'd be able to reach out and touch him. For a second, she considered looking away.

"What?" she said. Even to her own ears, she sounded defensive.

He just shook his head and winced, and she wasn't sure what to make of his expression. "So we're doing that, are we?" He glanced back to where Jessa had been, now long gone. "Are we going to do that thing where you say you don't know what I'm talking about? Because we both know that's bullshit. You're here to, what, confront her over a lie from years ago? How does it matter anymore, Suzanne?"

The way he said it, she didn't think she could've explained to anyone how much it bothered her.

"How can you say that?" she said. "Of course I'm going to ask her, confront her. If she lied, I want her to admit it to my face. She owes me that much."

"If she lied?" He leaned in, and she could feel how bad it must have sounded. He seemed ready to be done with her and walk away.

"Okay, bad choice of words. I didn't mean it like that. I want to stand in front of her and see her face when I tell her I know what she did. I want to find out from her why she would lie like that. She was my best friend, and she destroyed that. Coming to me the way she did, telling me you'd slept with her, she cried real tears, begging for my forgiveness. I was gutted, and I can't quite rationalize why she'd do that. I still don't get it." She could feel the heave in her chest as she breathed out.

He crossed his arms, and his biceps oozed strength. She couldn't pull her gaze from him. What was it about this Harold that was so different from the young man she'd been head over heels for?

"So is this about setting the record straight, or is it really that you're wondering who's telling the truth? Are we still doing that, Suzanne? You know what? Don't answer that. I can tell by your face that's exactly what this is. So then what? Seriously, Suzanne, what is this really about? When you learn the truth, will you want an apology? Because I can still see the doubt there. Don't deny it. You just can't believe that someone could so easily tell a lie." He gestured toward her, then rested his hands on his duty belt.

She wished he wouldn't do that. There was just something about the way he moved, the way he looked, that was making her feel things she hadn't expected.

She couldn't get her tongue to move, and when he went to step away, what did she do but reach over and touch his arm? His eyes went right to her hand, and she slowly pulled it away, knowing her mistake. Yeah, touching him was also confusing the hell out of her.

"She was my best friend, Harold," she said. "You're right about me wanting to set the record straight. At the same time, I'm angry over a lot of things about this. I believed her, and she crushed me. We were never close again after that, considering I saw her on your arm next. You say she asked you to the prom, but you took her. Yeah, I should have said something, but you know what? At the time, I was gutted, because I couldn't believe you'd toss me away like that. I never wanted to talk to you again after.

"Maybe I'm having trouble getting my head around the fact that I've believed a lie for so long, and then, all of a sudden, I find out what could be the truth. You want to point out to me how I should've said something to you when it happened? Fine, go ahead, you're right. Wouldn't life be so much easier if we could all have a do-over? But we can't. All we have is now, here, and I want answers. I want her to look me in the eye and explain to me how she could have done that, why she did what she did, and, even after all these years, why she's never come clean. Doesn't she have a conscience, knowing she destroyed us…?"

Harold made a rude noise and shook his head, glancing to the side and back to her. She could see he wasn't getting it—or maybe he was. "Suzanne, she didn't destroy us. You did when you believed something that wasn't true. We could go on and on and rehash this over and over, but it's going nowhere. Again, I asked you why it matters now. Years have gone past. We're done and over this, or you should be, at least, because I am. Anyway, aren't you involved with Lieutenant Chandler?"

She inhaled, trying to figure out what to say, then shrugged. "Honestly, I don't know where Toby and I stand. That's the truth, Harold, but it has nothing to do with this. I'm angry."

He didn't nod, and she wasn't sure what to make of the way he was looking at her now, but he gave her everything. She wanted him to say something, but he didn't.

"So Jessa said you have a suspect for the fire?" she finally said, pressing her hand to her chest. This back and forth about her and Harold and what could have been was making her damn uncomfortable, considering the way she had pictured their lives together back then. They would get married, have kids, have a life, yet they had become two very different people.

"We're investigating. Arson is suspected, but you should know that. Fire department investigators were in there and issued a preliminary report. Your boss would have it—but you don't, do you?"

She just shrugged, wondering what boss he was talking about, the chief or Toby. Likely both. Under normal circumstances, she wouldn't necessarily know. "Toby and I aren't on good terms right now. He's benched me until I get a doctor's okay to go back to work, and he's up for another promotion to captain." She couldn't believe the way she'd said it, and she didn't miss his wince.

"Ouch," was all he said.

She wondered why she would've shared this with him. "Yeah, well, I made my feelings clear and called out his bullshit, his screw-up last night, how he shouldn't be promoted. Apparently, he didn't want to hear the truth, so yeah, here I am, sidelined…" She gestured to herself and tried to make light of it, but instead she felt like shit. "Sorry. I shouldn't be ragging on him."

Harold nodded and glanced away. She wasn't sure what was there in his expression. He was a different person now, and she had no idea how to read him.

"No, you shouldn't. You're involved with him, so work it out with him. Captain, really? Scary. At the same time, I hear you on why you're disagreeing with how everything went down. That promotion shouldn't happen, but be careful, Suzanne, because it sounds like you're mixing business, pleasure, and politics, and the one who could end up getting burned is you. You've been benched...?" He shook his head.

She wasn't sure whether he agreed with what had happened or not, and she was feeling as if she was about to be scolded for something.

"Well, that's a shitty thing," he finally said, "but you're dealing with different personalities, and that's why they frown on workplace romance. You could file a grievance, but I've seen this kind of thing before, and even if things go your way, in the end, they won't. Just my two cents, though. You can take what you want from it. At the same time, if I were you, I would get real clear on your relationship with the lieutenant, because if that's what you want to work out, you may need to dial back on your criticism. The guy I met last night gave me the impression that he wouldn't handle that kind of thing very well, in my opinion."

He reached over, pressed his hand to her arm, and rubbed, then stepped back and slipped his shades back on. "Enjoy your time off," was all he said before he inclined his head and started walking away to City Hall, up the steps, where she'd been headed moments ago. He didn't look back.

As that giant empty hole filled her stomach and chest, she realized that her feelings had everything to do with Harold, a man she'd believed had deceived her. He was right about one thing she needed to figure out: Where exactly did all of this put her relationship with Toby?

Chapter 12

Not only was there an email in her inbox, an official letter from Lieutenant Toby Chandler, outlining her time off for the rest of the week, but she couldn't believe he'd actually added in the instruction for her to be cleared by a doctor.

She stared at the email, which had dinged on her phone as she passed the sheriff's office, having decided to walk the few blocks from City Hall to the firehall. Evidently, that had been a bad idea, considering Toby was still smarting over her having pointed out that he wasn't qualified to be her boss. What really pissed her off was the fact that he was messing with her job, her career, something she loved and was really good at, over what? He was taking this very personally.

She just shook her head, pulled up Toby's name on her cell, and dialed his number. It rang twice, three times, then went to voicemail: "Hey, this is Lieutenant Toby Chandler. I'm likely on the job right now, so leave a message and I'll get right back to you. Have a great day." More than likely, he'd seen her name on the screen and was too chickenshit to talk to her.

"Asshole!" she muttered, then waited for the beep to start her message. "I'm pretty sure you know damn well who this is, considering you just fired off an official request that's absolute bullshit. You know I'm fine. You're just pissed because I spoke up and said what no one else has the guts to say…"

She stopped talking when she heard the beep, realizing she'd been cut off. She pulled the phone away and stared at it before hitting the end button. She couldn't remember ever having felt quite so helpless as this. This was cruel and underhanded. She wanted to go head to head with him, and she took one step and then another before making herself stop, taking in the steps up to the sheriff's office.

She started up them and pulled open the glass door, and before she could consider what she was doing, she was walking inside. She heard the phones, saw where Charlotte sat with her long dark hair pinned up, wearing a deputy's uniform, and Colby sat at another desk, on the phone. And her brother? Where he was, she didn't know.

"Suzanne, what brings you by?" Charlotte said, stuffing a file into the old filing cabinet.

Suzanne took in the two other empty desks and wondered which of them belonged to Harold.

"Heard about last night from Marcus," Charlotte continued. "He was sure worried about you."

She really did have a calming way about her. With her and Marcus together, seeing them now, Suzanne couldn't shake the sense of how right they seemed, as if they'd always been together.

"Is Marcus in?" she said. She couldn't shake the awkward feeling, which was silly.

Charlotte glanced over to the closed door of his office.

"He's in with Lonnie. Not sure how long he'll be," she said, then gestured to her desk before glancing over her shoulder to Colby, who was still on the phone. "You know what? I'm sure he won't be much longer. I could poke my head in and let him know you're here."

Suzanne could see she was trying, but she couldn't shake the sense of feeling so out of place. She wondered if Harold would walk in. Maybe this wasn't such a good idea. Charlotte reached over and rested her hand on her arm when she didn't answer.

"No, don't bother him," Suzanne said. "I can wait a minute. It's nothing urgent. Just had the day off and was in the neighborhood…"

Charlotte lifted a brow. Of course, it sounded like an excuse, considering she never just dropped by at the sheriff's office because she was in the neighborhood, not really.

"Okay, that sounded really pathetic, didn't it?" she said.

Charlotte seemed to consider something, and then an odd smile touched her lips. "You know if you need something or just want to bend Marcus's ear, you don't have to explain yourself to me. I know he'd be happy to see you, and it's okay to stop in. You don't need a reason. I'm sure Marcus would be happy just to see you're all right. I know he was worried about you and Harold being trapped back there in the fire. He was pretty angry with Toby, too. Apparently they got into it last night a little bit…" She bit her lip as if she'd said something she shouldn't have.

"I'm fine," Suzanne said. "I barely breathed any smoke, just a little. Harold was more affected. My trip to the hospital was routine. They checked me over, and I was home a few hours later. So what happened between my brother and Toby?"

Charlotte glanced over to the closed door of the sheriff's office. "Oh, they had a conversation, something about him screwing up last night and the fact that things could've ended far worse than they did, and his incompetence could've cost you your life, that kind of thing. Sorry. I know you and Toby have a thing and all and are together, but I'm with Marcus on this. When he told me about the calls Toby made, how you were trapped in that back room, we realized that if it hadn't been for Kyle pulling everyone in and using every resource to put out the fire and get you out…"

The door opened, and she heard her brother and Lonnie as they stepped out into the bullpen, still talking. She didn't miss the surprise on his face when he saw her.

"Suzanne, didn't know you were coming by," Marcus said. He walked over to them and handed Charlotte a file, and she saw the chemistry between them, the caring in their relationship, which did seem to work, even here at the office.

"Yeah, I, uh, was just in the neighborhood…"

Marcus glanced down to Charlotte, who was giving him everything, and Suzanne saw something unspoken between them. "Come on in," he said. "Wanted to see how you were, anyway. You saved me a phone call." He tilted his head toward the office. "Was going to check in…"

She followed him into his office and closed the door, taking in Bert's old desk, which Marcus had now taken over. It didn't appear that he'd changed anything: the same dated coat rack, the same old maps on the wall.

Marcus stopped talking and was now leaning against his desk, crossing his arms. He hadn't shaved, and she wondered, after last night, how much sleep he'd had.

"So, I heard you got into it with Toby," she said. Was that really what she wanted to know? No. She was still reeling from having been sidelined over something beyond her control, on grounds that were completely invalid. She was pacing, and it wasn't lost on her how Marcus's eyes tracked her.

"So you're here because of Toby," he said.

She shook out her arms, feeling so unsettled. "No, I was seriously out front, about ready to walk on down to the firehall, when Toby sent me an email benching me officially after we had a fight this morning. I figured I should take a minute and calm down before I made things worse."

Marcus just raised his brows, maybe surprised. "Benched you for what?" he said. There it was, the tone he used when Toby's name came up.

"Did you know that Toby has been offered or is about to be given a promotion to captain?" she said. She could tell by Marcus's face that he hadn't heard.

He made a rude noise and then pressed his thumb and finger to the bridge of his nose. "Let me guess: The chief was behind it. Wow. I don't even know what to say to that. First lieutenant and now captain? I seriously hope you can see it now."

She didn't miss the accusation, the anger that always seemed to simmer just below the surface, showing how much he despised Toby. If there was anyone her brother was never going to give a pass to, Toby was definitely that person.

"When he showed up this morning, thinking I'd be happy for him over the news, I may have outlined how he screwed up last night at the fire. But you already know that. What's worse is that he can't see it, and he didn't appreciate my commenting on the real reason he got the promotion, which is because of his grandfather, not because he earned it. Now I'm on a week's holiday, and he wants a doctor's note before I can go back to work. To add insult to injury, he just emailed me officially." She went to pull her phone from her purse, then dropped her hand. "I'm ranting, but I figured it was best to come in here and vent to you instead of making a fool of myself at the firehall, where it could be used against me and would likely have me benched permanently."

Marcus didn't seem impressed and was shaking his head. "Please let this mean that you're done with him and see how he's not worth your time. That's all I ask. And you're right: You can stop in and vent anytime."

What could she say? She was furious with Toby, but at the same time, after the night before, everything about her and Toby had suddenly become more complicated.

She didn't answer the question. Instead, she said, "So I ran into Harold a bit ago outside City Hall. I see he's working today. How's he doing?"

From the way Marcus narrowed his eyes, she could see his interest. "Harold is fine. He was told to take it easy, but he said he's good, and that's good enough for me. So what's the deal with you two? And don't say it's nothing, Suzanne. I watched you both last night. Did something happen that I should know about?"

There it was, the scenario between her and Harold, which had also become more complicated.

Just then, there was a knock at the door, and it popped open.

"Sheriff, I just got word that they found the surveillance video…" Harold poked his head in and stopped talking when he saw her. He nodded and opened the door, fully stepping in. "Sorry. I didn't mean to interrupt."

"No, it's fine," Marcus said as he stood, stepping away from the desk and giving everything to Harold, who was now so close to her. She didn't know what expression was on her face, and she couldn't pull her gaze from him. "What was that about the surveillance video?"

Harold glanced her way for only a second. "In the store, from the cameras before the fire. The store security indicated they had a suspect, whom they were watching. He appeared nervous, and they suspected he was up to no good, as the manager put it. They're sending video surveillance over for us to see. The arson investigator has indicated in a preliminary report to the mayor that it likely started in a couple spots, clothing and sporting goods. I said you'd want to look at it."

She wondered how much of this Toby already knew. All of it, likely. She was out of the loop, and she crossed her arms over her chest, feeling so out of place. "So it was arson," she said, more to herself than anything.

Marcus gestured to Harold and didn't look her way. "Let me know as soon as the video shows up so we can figure out who this suspect is. I'd love to have this closed down instead of starting a long, drawn-out investigation."

Harold nodded to her and then turned and started out of the office, but he stopped in the doorway for just a second. "Suzanne," was all he said.

She found herself just staring at the open door after he walked away. She heard her brother clear his throat, and she turned back to him and took in the open question on his face, which was unmistakable.

"You mind telling me what that was about?" he said. From his expression, for a second, she didn't know what he was talking about. When she didn't say anything, he stepped over to her and looked down at her, then over to the open door where Harold had been. "Maybe there is hope for you, after all," he added, as if considering something. Then he pulled in a breath. "Right, you and Harold were an item in high school, huh... Just remember, Suzanne, he's a good guy."

"I don't know what you're talking about," Suzanne

said, not liking the direction he was going with this. "It was a long time ago. There's nothing between us anymore."

Marcus shook his head. "Really? Maybe you want to tell yourself that, because the way you're watching him isn't saying there's nothing. Take it from someone who knows you, Suzanne."

For a second, she was about to deny it, but Marcus cut her off.

"Harold is a good guy," he said. "If you want him, fine, but don't mess with my deputy. He's good at what he does. With you being angry at Toby and him pulling this stupid-ass shit, maybe I should thank him, because the only thing I want for you, Suzanne, is for you to stop making excuses for Toby Chandler and see him for who he is."

Her brother's gaze lingered another second in that way that said he thought he knew something, and she knew it was now time to go.

Chapter 13

She took in the red shiny firetruck, which Kyle was washing down by hand from a soap bucket. The doors of the firehall were open, and she heard voices inside. Her hair was hanging long and loose, and she had opted for casual blue jeans and a white T-shirt. Her hands were sweating, and she felt awkward in a way that was silly. As she looked up at the firehall, the red brick, the windows, Kyle lifted his hand and called out to her. She couldn't shake this sense that things would never be the same again. She loved this place, being a firefighter. It was just one of those things she knew she was born to do.

"Toby in?" she asked as she stepped up to the doors.

Kyle just gestured to the upstairs window as he fired the hose to rinse off the firetruck. She kept going into the firehouse and heard voices from the back kitchen, but she didn't bother going in to say hi to anyone. That wasn't why she was there. She wouldn't allow herself to become distracted as she started up the stairs.

It had been two days since Toby had fired off that email and three days since she'd been eating her heart out because he was stringing her along. She spotted him behind his desk, doing paperwork, she supposed. As she tapped on the door, she took in his surprise when he looked up and over to her. He leaned back in his chair, and it squeaked.

"Suzanne, what are you doing here?" He gestured toward her before tossing down the pen he was holding. "I told you to take the week off."

She didn't miss how cool he was in the way he watched her. He didn't pull his gaze from her, and there was nothing fun and flirty there. She reached into her purse and pulled out an envelope to toss onto his desk.

His hand rested on it. "What's this?" He held it up.

She stepped into the office, leaving the door open. "What you asked for, a doctor's note, remember? You want official, there it is. I'm all cleared to return to work."

He gave the envelope a toss without bothering to look at it, considering the trouble he'd made her go to. She'd visited her family doctor for a quick exam, then had to pay two hundred bucks just for the signed letter.

"You're still off for the week," he said, closing the file he was looking at.

"Is this my punishment for talking to you the way I did?" she said. "Or are you wanting me to apologize? Because an apology isn't coming."

This time, he slid back his chair and strode past her to give the door a shove closed, then walked to the window. She could see the way he fisted his hands. Evidently, that happy loving feeling for her was gone. So it was that easy. He crossed his arms and leaned against the window. There was something about Toby: When someone pissed him off, he made no attempt to hide it.

"I'm not punishing you," he said. "Is that what you think this is?"

Was he serious?

He pushed away from the window and ran his hands through his thick dark hair. "You scared the shit out of me, Suzanne, what you did in the fire. I always thought you had my back. What's really going on with you and this Harold Waters?"

She just stared at him, wondering where this was coming from. "There's nothing between me and Harold. And about what happened in the fire, we've already been through this, so let's not rehash it. Harold and I dated in high school, years ago, just like I'm sure you've dated many women before me. This has everything to do with how you took your personal feelings and brought them into this firehall." She strode over to his desk and picked up the envelope he'd tossed to the side, setting it in the center of his desk and jabbing it with her middle finger. "This may be a joke to you, but it cost me two hundred dollars and time away from a job I love, all because I've, what, stepped on your ego? I won't apologize for that. Toby, this silent treatment is ridiculous and juvenile. Two days ago, I called you, and yeah, I left you a pissed-off message, but I had a right to be furious. You never even had the decency to call me back." She shrugged and didn't know what to make of the way he was watching her.

"Maybe I overreacted," he said, starting toward her. There was something in the way he was looking at her, the way his voice had softened. It had her feeling uncomfortable. He was so handsome, so drop-dead gorgeous, and it really did cloud her good sense.

"Maybe? You did overreact. You overstepped, Toby. You abused your authority, and you belittled me. That's not something you do to someone you supposedly care about."

He glanced away. She could see she was making him uncomfortable. Good!

"You asked me about us the other night before the fire," he said. "You wanted me to put a label on this thing we have, and I know I danced around it, but you have to know why."

This time, he gave everything to her. His blue eyes weren't filled with the usual teasing mischief that had her wanting to do anything for him. They were suddenly serious, too serious. She could feel the desk behind her. The uneasiness in her chest was building to something that was so damn uncomfortable. She wasn't sure she wanted to hear what he had to say.

"You know, Toby, you don't have to explain. I know I push at times, and you're right; you made it clear you wanted nothing serious. I get it."

He was shaking his head. "Just listen to me. It's not that. I've never met anyone like you, Suzanne. Nothing scares you, you're confident… Look at you. You take things head on and don't care what anyone thinks. You're smart as all hell, but at the same time, every time we're together, it both excites me and terrifies me."

She didn't know what to say to that.

He took another step closer to her. "When you asked me where I was for those two hours, I knew you knew that I was blowing you off, but it isn't as you think. Yes, I was with someone…"

"I don't want to hear this." She cut him off and lifted her hand, then started to walk past him, but he reached out and grabbed her arm and stopped her.

"Well, you're going to hear it. I was at the Lighthouse with a few of the guys here, and I met a woman. I bought her a drink and flirted, and of course she was all ready to go back to my place or hers, but when she went to kiss me, there was something about it…" He shook his head. "She wasn't you, and I was furious with myself and you, because I knew, even though I wouldn't admit it, that I was in love with you, and the last time I allowed myself to fall for a girl, give my heart to her, she shredded it, and I swore, never again." He let go of her arm and stepped away, shaking his head, looking up at the ceiling. He paced in a circle back over to the window, and she was too stunned to say anything. At the same time, she wasn't sure what he expected from her.

"So what is this?" she said, glancing back to the closed door.

Toby looked down and then over to her. "I don't want to lose you, Suzanne. I'll just put it out there. I love you. You wanted an answer, you've got it. You scare the hell out of me, but worse is that when you went into that fire and I was outside that store, knowing you were inside that building, all I could think of was getting you out. You criticized how I handled things? Get in line. I already heard it from Kyle too, and my grandfather. So evidently you're not the only one who thinks I fucked up. But the thing is, Suzanne, I can't be a good leader with you here. After giving you the week off and not having you here, I realized that if something were to happen, something serious, and we got a call, I could handle the situation with a clear head because you weren't there."

She stared at Toby and realized what he was saying. "You're firing me, aren't you."

He glanced away. There he went, hiding his feelings, though he'd completely pulled the rug out from under her and gutted her.

"I guess you didn't hear me," he said. "I love you, but I don't want to work with you."

Chapter 14

Suzanne lay on her back on the concrete underneath her jacked-up MGB, giving everything she had to loosening the stuck plug so she could change the oil, even though she'd changed it not even three months earlier. It was the only thing she could think to do aside from taking her engine apart and putting it back together, trying to come to terms with how she'd basically been hung out to dry.

She finally reached for the mallet and whacked the end of her wrench until it gave and she could loosen the bolt. She slid the pan under before pulling out the plug, letting the black oil pour out.

She heard a knock on the open door of her garage, and she held the wrench, looking over and seeing feet, men's feet, wearing black boots.

When she pushed herself out and looked up, there was Harold staring down at her—in amusement, she thought. He lifted his gaze and took in her single-car garage, which was the only thing about her small older house that she loved.

"So this is where you hang out," he said. "Marcus said you've created the ideal man cave, or rather woman cave, and you spend more time under the hood of your car than is normal for a woman."

He stepped into the garage. Along one wall was a bench she'd built with a metal shelf and every tool a home mechanic would use. She wasn't sure what to make of the way he was looking at her.

"You have grease on your face," he said and gestured.

She sat up on the concrete, taking in her grease-stained old torn-at-the-knee jeans and her faded blue and red shirt, which was also smudged. Her hands were dirty, but being clean in a garage was just something that didn't happen.

"What are you doing here?" she said, still sitting there, holding her wrench. She put it down beside her on the concrete when he held out a hand to help her up. "You sure you want to do that? I'll get you dirty." She held up her hands, showing him the grease. She had no problem admitting to anyone that this was her happy place.

He said nothing for a second. "It's just dirt. It washes off. Come on." He reached down, taking her hand and pulling her up with little effort.

She took in his casual side, blue jeans and a faded gray T-shirt. She noted his badge tucked over the waistband of his jeans and his holstered gun. "So is this a casual day on the job, or are you off duty?"

This was just something she wasn't used to seeing from the town deputies. She brushed back a lock of her hair that had fallen free from her ponytail.

His amber eyes hinted at his amusement. "I'm always on the job. Never knew you had such a love of mechanics. Marcus says you've basically rebuilt this car from scratch."

What could she say? It was just something she'd fallen into. Some people took up gardening or renovations; she had taken up automotive repair. There was just something about tinkering in her car, working with tools, that gave her a sense of peace. She knew many wouldn't understand.

She reached for a cloth from the top of the car and wiped her hands. She didn't know why she was so uncomfortable in this silence with Harold, who she had to remind herself had never been a chatty guy. She'd always done all the talking, and he'd listened.

Maybe he was waiting for her to say something as he walked around her garage, taking in her car.

"Yeah, this is my baby," she finally said. "So, you didn't answer me when I asked you why you're here. And how did you know where I live, anyway?"

He lifted a socket wrench and then her old clutch from the workbench and took them in, then set both down before walking around the car to her. "Finding people is what I do. I'm a cop. But Marcus told me where you were."

He stopped right in front of her, and she took in his arms, his chest, and the way he walked. There was just something about him, how buff he was and the way he carried himself. She couldn't help but watch him. He allowed his gaze to drop, taking her in, and she fought the urge to cross her arms as she stood before him. He had a way of going deep, the distance, not keeping her at arm's length.

"Wanted to check on you, see how you're doing," he said, not pulling his gaze, giving everything to her. She wondered how much he knew. Everything, likely.

"So you heard that my job with the department is basically gone. My week off is likely to be permanent, and I'm sitting at home, awaiting my fate. I'm basically fighting an uphill battle to get my job back after someone I cared about very much decided he could just yank it away."

He didn't nod but finally looked away, pulling a breath before giving everything to her. "Yeah, heard they're looking for a fall guy for the fire. Word traveled that you're out. You should know that Marcus is fighting it from his end. He won't stand for it, but he also doesn't have much leeway in the jurisdiction of the fire department. He's gone to the mayor to fight for you, but at the same time…" He shook his head, and she had a sinking feeling she wasn't going to want to hear this.

"You know it's Toby behind this," she said. "How can a man who says he loves me basically destroy my career to protect himself?" She knew he didn't get it by the way his expression turned hard and confused. "Yeah, that was exactly what he said to me. I took him the required doctor's note, and he said that having me with the depart-ment is too much of a distraction for him, that he can't think clearly with me around, and because of me, he couldn't make the right calls at the fire. He said the few days I wasn't there were basically the deciding factor in him tossing me away like I'm garbage. What does that say about his role as a leader if he can't separate his feelings from the job…?"

Harold settled his hands over his waistband of his jeans and seemed to be considering something. She wondered if he agreed. "The fire was a big deal, but you know that," he said. "It's about the dollars, city taxes that still have to be collected, and the fact that someone has to take the blame. They want a fall guy. The store is closed for months, and people are out of work, so they need someone accountable on paper. It doesn't matter who it is. I was at the scene, and so were other firefighters, but it's Toby Chandler and the chief who are meeting with City Council. This is when you see no one wanting to step up and say what really went down. Yeah, you're right that Toby screwed up and made some bad calls, but no one is willing to say so. They want their jobs. They don't want their heads on the chopping block."

She wondered if Harold being here was an official warning, maybe a heads-up.

"So where exactly does this leave you and Toby?" he said.

She wasn't sure what to make of that, considering she'd walked out of Toby's office the day before and hadn't spoken to him since he'd said he loved her and then basically fired her. Who did that? Toby, evidently. It had given her a close-up view of who he really was. She'd ignored his six phone calls and deleted his voicemails without listening to them.

"I guess news travels fast, doesn't it? So everyone knows that we were involved? Let me emphasize *were*, as in past tense. You ask where this leaves me and Toby..." She shrugged. "Where do you think? Nowhere. You really expect that I could be with someone who could toss me away that easily and rip away something that I love, then in the next breath say he loves me? It's shitty and wrong. You know I trained him, but evidently not well. So in case I didn't answer you, there is no Toby and me. If I'm being honest with myself, there never really was."

She pulled in a breath, feeling so many things as she stood there with Harold, waiting for him to say anything that could make this better. She felt as if the world and everything she knew wasn't how she'd thought it was just a week earlier.

"Well, he's a fool, and it's his loss. At the same time, you can't hide out here and just wait for someone to decide something. This is your life someone's screwing with, Suzanne."

"I realize that, but what am I supposed to do when the

deck is stacked against me?" She gestured to herself, at a loss.

"File a grievance before the board. Order an investigation. Fight this. Don't just lie down and take it. You're right about one thing: When a man loves a woman, he doesn't mess with her career just because he can't keep his head screwed on and separate the personal from the professional. He had a job to do and didn't do it. Then there's his promotion to captain. There's no way you should want that to happen. As much as I'd like to fight this for you, this is your fight."

The way he said it, the way he was looking at her, she wished so many things hadn't happened. She felt the what-if nipping at her.

"I've made a lot of mistakes," she said, "but you know what the biggest regret is, the thing I wish I could go back and undo?"

He didn't say anything. He gently shook his head, and she wondered if he knew.

"I wish I never listened to Jessa," she said. "I wish I'd called her out. I wish I had gone to you about her lie. Out of all that's happened, that's the one thing out of this that I regret. Do you ever wonder where we'd be right now...?"

He stepped closer and lifted his hand, pressing his fingers over her cheek and brushing back her hair. He was so close that she could feel everything about him, and it was calming. "You can spend your entire life with regrets and what-ifs, but the fact remains, Suzanne, you believed her. Neither of us could know where you and I would be right now, whether we'd even be together. It could've been something else or someone else for either of us. I don't know that, and you don't know that. What I do know is the council is meeting this afternoon. Marcus is going to be there, and so are the chief and Toby. You need to be there, Suzanne. Only you can fight for your job."

He leaned in and pressed a kiss to her lips. It was so tender, and he stepped back and took another look around her garage, pressing his hand to the side of her head before looking at her again.

"Think about it," was all he said before he stepped around her and started out of the garage.

"Harold…" she called out.

He turned, taking her in. "Yeah?"

"Thanks for everything."

Chapter 15

Walking into City Hall, she wore her blue work uniform, her hair tied back. She'd scrubbed the grease from her hands the best she could.

She took in Jessa Armstrong, who was walking down the stairs in heels and a cream pantsuit with a red silky blouse. She hesitated when she spotted Suzanne, and for a second, Suzanne thought she was about to turn and race back up the stairs. It was ridiculous, so what did she do but stand there at the bottom of those stairs and give her everything?

"Jessa, do you have a minute?" she called. She took in the woman she was now, the woman she'd loved so deeply at one time, her best friend from so long ago, until, one moment, she wasn't anymore.

"Well, I have to get into chambers for that meeting, so I don't really have a minute, actually—but we should catch up. Why don't you call my assistant and see that she gets you on the books?" The way she said it was an unmistakeable tell of how nervous she was.

"No, actually, this won't take long, Jessa." She stepped

in front of her. Only a fool could've missed how on edge she was.

Jessa lifted her wrist, looking at her watch. "Only a minute, Suzanne. I have responsibilities. What is it?"

"I wanted to ask you something about Harold. Do you remember when you came to me and said that you slept with my boyfriend and then begged for my forgiveness? You even cried. I have to know why you did it."

She made a face and gestured vaguely. Her blue eyes glanced away, then pulled back to her. "Look, that was a long time ago, Suzanne, and who's to say what really happened? Maybe I don't quite remember it that way."

She took a step into her space. She couldn't believe she'd said that. Maybe her expression said as much, as Jessa hesitated. This was one of the two people who had messed with her life, and that thought was getting to her.

"Don't lie to me, not me," she said.

Jessa sighed. "Look, Harold already came at me over that. I'm sorry. I'll tell you the same thing I told him. It was a stupid move, and maybe I did bend the truth just a bit, but it was high school and a long time ago. We're grown-ups now. I'm married. Haven't we all moved on?" She reached over and rubbed her hand on Suzanne's arm as if they were friends, as if she cared. "I'm sorry, Suzanne," she said, really emphasizing the point. "But really, what does it matter now? You did things, too, if you really want to get into it. You weren't the greatest of friends." She lifted her wrist again. "Look, I really have to get in there."

"You said Harold talked with you already." She wondered if she'd heard her right.

Jessa just rolled her eyes. "Yes, he showed up at my office and called me out over my little fib. I'm sorry. He was a little mad, but as I said to him, it was ages ago. We all did things as kids that were really dumb, and that was mine. I'm caught, it's out. No, we didn't sleep together." She stopped talking and let out a sigh before looking up to her and then past her. "Look, Suzanne, I feel bad, okay? But at the same time, you should know he really cares about you. The way he came into my office, the way he's fought for your job…"

"Wait, what?" she cut in, holding her hands up. "What do you mean, he fought for me? What are you talking about?"

Jessa smiled and shook her head dramatically. "I can see when a man loves a woman. Harold has feelings for you. He's fought for your job with the fire department, saying you were railroaded, the fall guy, and he's going to bat for you. I've never seen that before. When a man is willing to fight like Harold is for you, despite the fact that fingers were being pointed your way, people saying you didn't follow orders and you're about to be officially fired… He won't stand for it. He asked—no, demanded that I back you up. He said I owe you."

Suzanne just stared at her, not knowing what to say.

A slow smile touched Jessa's lips. "He's right; I do owe you. And another thing, Suzanne. No one really believes you should be the fall guy, but at the same time, so many questions are being asked about why the fire wasn't put out quickly, why more couldn't be done to save the store so people could get back to work in weeks rather than months. They want someone to blame. Even though I understand they have a suspect and the official report is arson, tossing you under the bus seems to have satisfied the mayor and a few of the other city councillors."

"So where do you stand, Jessa? Are you going to sit back and see to it that I lose my job and this is pinned on me?"

She narrowed her eyes, leaned in, and lowered her

voice. "Suzanne, I may have lied once, and it cost our friendship, but I'm not about to sit back and watch you be railroaded. And one more thing…" Jessa glanced past her and tapped her arm so she turned to look, seeing that Marcus and Harold were standing just outside the chambers, talking and looking her way. "That man has feelings for you." Jessa looked at her watch again. "I have to go."

She started walking, her heels clicking on the floor, echoing. She called out and lifted her hand in a wave to both Marcus and Harold. Just then, Suzanne spotted Toby walking in with the chief and a man she recognized as his grandfather.

She started walking, and Toby must have seen her, as he said something to them and then started her way. Damn, he was still good looking, but there was something about him, as she glanced over to Harold, that just didn't sit right with her. She stopped where she was and took in the way he looked right and then left before he approached her, a motion she knew well.

"I heard you filed an official grievance," he said. Was that anger in his voice?

"You took my job and are trying to make me the fall guy," she said. "Of course I did."

He let out a rough, frustrated breath and shook his head, letting his gaze dip to her. "You know this will be the end of us, then."

Why had she never seen this side of him?

"I think you're confused, Toby," she said. "There is no us."

He shook his head, and the smile that touched his lips was anything but friendly. His blue eyes rested on her again. "So that's the way you want to play it? I lay my heart out to you, and you can't even give a little. I have a great opportunity that you'll never have, Suzanne. Fine, you want to make this a fight?" He shook his head, and she just stared at him.

Harold was walking her way, and Marcus was now talking with the chief. She wasn't sure where Toby's grandfather had gone.

"No, Toby, I don't want to fight you, but I will, because I'm not about to give up something I love, my dream of being a firefighter, just because a fall guy is needed. You toss words at me, saying you love me, but honestly, I don't think you know what love is. I think you love yourself more."

"Everything all right here?" Harold said as he strode around Toby and came to stand right beside her. There was just something about the motion, about him, that said everything to her.

Toby lifted his hands as if he was done, then stepped back. The expression on his face was one she'd not seen often. "No, I'm done here," he said, then walked away without a glance back to her.

She couldn't believe he could be so cruel. It hurt. She hadn't realized she was shaking, but Harold must have known, as he took her hand. She flicked her gaze over to him. Something about the motion had settled her.

"So you're really going to fight this," he said, then pulled his hand away. Everything about him was so grounded. How had she missed that?

"Well, someone I really care about gave me some good advice, and I'd have to be a fool not to listen to it."

He didn't smile, but light touched his amber eyes, and it eased the nervousness that had kicked up inside her. Within moments, she would go into a room where her fate would be decided. He had to know how she felt.

"Is this someone I know?" he said.

She slid her hand over his arm, feeling his strength. "I think you know it is."

He said nothing, though she sensed he wanted to. The doors to the council chamber opened, but she just wanted to stand there with him for another moment.

He ran both his hands over her arms, her shoulders. "Just take a breath. Breathe, okay? I got your back." At the way he said it, she had to fight the tightness in her chest, the emotion that welled.

"I was a fool to let a lie come between us," she said. "Whatever Jessa said, it was my fault. I should never have believed her. I'm sorry that I never came to you, talked to you. I didn't have your back, but here you are." She shut her eyes for a second and felt his hands still there on her shoulders. He pressed a kiss to her forehead, then somehow had her turned, walking toward the chamber. "So whatever happens in there," she said, "I want you to know I wouldn't want anyone else here with me."

He just grunted, and as she looked up at him, she realized that just maybe, she would get that second chance.

Chapter 16

The door to her MGB squeaked as she stepped out, and the voices of her family drifted out of her brother Ryan's house. She took in Harold getting out from the other side, dressed in blue jeans and a faded dress shirt. His light hair had a soft wave. Everything about him settled her in ways she couldn't have explained to anyone.

"You sure you want to meet everyone?" she said. "They can be a handful, and they'll assume we're together, you know."

He walked over to her, rested his hands on her arms, and then took her hand in his. "Let them. Besides, you still haven't told your family about the board's ruling, have you?"

He knew she hadn't. What was she supposed to say? The fire department had been ordered to give her job back, but, not surprisingly, the position she'd held had been contracted out the day before the ruling came down. She was pissed, and Harold was furious, but that was the reality of how things worked.

She shook her head. "No. How do I tell everyone that the job I loved is gone? Yes, I can work for the next county over when they have an opening, but unfortunately, I got screwed over."

He slid his arm around her and pulled her closer, pressing a kiss to her forehead, then to her lips when she leaned against him and looked up. "Well, tell them exactly that, and then let it be. Let them be angry with you. As I told you, you lost the battle, not the war. Sometimes, you have to take a step back and see all of it. He will screw up. He'll do something that'll cost him. At the same time, could you have gone back and worked under him?"

She knew the "him" he was referring to was Toby, a man she'd been head over heels for, though everything she'd felt for him was now gone. "No, you're right, I couldn't have." How could she respect someone who could toss her away as Toby had? "But this here…" Her fingers were linked with his. Just touching him, being close to him, seemed natural and easy. For the first time in her life, she felt as if she'd been given a second chance to right a wrong. "This is all that's important. Let them rant and be angry for a moment, but this here, with us, you having my back, the way I feel about you… I guess I just want you to know, so there's no misunderstanding, Harold, that I once loved you so deeply. I guess what I'm saying is that those feelings never really went away."

She looked up to him, and he glanced over to the house as the screen door opened and Marcus stepped out.

Harold's hand settled around the small of her back, and he brought her closer. "Well, that's good, then. I guess that gives us something to talk about," he said. Then he laughed softly, leaned down, and kissed her.

Chapter 17

Suzanne took in Toby's faded brown T-shirt on top of her hamper and considered, just for a second, calling him. Then she'd, what, drive over there and return it to him?

"I think not," she said under her breath as she dumped it in the washer with the rest of her clothes. She'd wash it and add it to the pile she was planning on giving away to charity.

She heard a knock on the front door.

"Hello?" Karen called out. "I've never seen your front yard so neat. Didn't think you liked flowers."

Suzanne knew she was referring to the small front yard she'd previously let go. Now, with all her free time, she'd decided it could use some landscaping and had added a flower bed at the front of the house, along with two planter boxes below the front window, with marigolds, asters, and a small white rose bush that would hopefully climb the side of the house. Maybe next week she'd think about painting the trim from ugly brown to something with curbside appeal, teal or maybe red.

Karen poked her head in the small laundry area by the back door off the tiny kitchen. She was wearing a bright fuchsia cotton dress with a cream-colored sweater overtop, with bare legs and wedged sandals, and her hair was deep mahogany now, hanging long and loose.

"There you are. Did you hear me?" she said, taking in the laundry. As Suzanne stepped out, the loud whir of the washer started.

"Yup, sorry. Doing laundry, is all. And yes, I figured with all this time on my hands, I could at least spruce this place up, considering being out of work means no paycheck, so I may need to put it on the market and sell it before the bank decides to take it from me because I can't pay the mortgage." She sounded grumpy even to herself, but then, she was out of a job she loved.

"Well, that's what I want to talk to you about. I know you said you wanted to lie low for a bit, but I really think you should reconsider and let me file a suit against the department."

Suzanne kept walking past her sister into the tiny kitchen, where she pulled open the fridge before closing it, opting to go right to the freezer. She reached for the tub of chocolate raspberry ice cream and lifted the lid only to see it was basically empty aside from a little bit she'd have to scrape to make even a teaspoon. She dumped it in the sink and glanced back at her sister, who didn't pull those O'Connell blue eyes from her.

"No, I don't want to file a suit against the fire depart-ment," she said. "I told you that already, in case you've forgotten. I'd like to be a firefighter again, but deciding to sue for any reason is the same as ensuring I'll never work in any department anywhere. As you already pointed out to me, either the chief, Toby's grandfather, or Toby himself was tipped off by someone on the council that they'd be ruling in my favor on the grievance and ordering the department to give me back my job, so they filled my position by hiring Everett full time, with benefits, the day before the official ruling. He was one of the volunteers, and he lacks any real firefighting experience. Then every one of my so-called 'brothers in blue,'" she said, complete with finger quotes, "refused to back me, because they all want to stay on the right side of this to save their own skins. Now Everett has my job, and they can't fire him or un-take the position from him, so no, it totally sucks, and I'm still furious and pissed, but I'm not suing. Albeit I won the grievance, I didn't really, because the strings are held by someone I've managed to piss off."

"Ah, I see you're still in that place, are you?" Karen said, having pulled her sunglasses off and rested them atop her head.

"Look, Karen, I know you're trying to help, but didn't you hear what both Marcus and Harold said about this? Even though I'd love nothing more than to jam up the chief, Toby, and his grandfather, this isn't something I'm going to win. Because even if by some miracle a court were to rule and pass down a nice payout for me, order them to give me a job, you know the system isn't going to work with me. If I did end up back on the job, it wouldn't be for long, because they'd find a way to pin something more serious on me, have anonymous complaints suddenly appearing about things I didn't do, and then things would start to stick, and they could say, 'See? We were right.' I wouldn't see it coming. I would have to watch my own back because no one would have mine at a fire. If I suddenly find myself trapped again, no one would come and save my ass. So no, Karen, as much as I'd love to, because what they did is so wrong and unfair and basically violates all my rights as a woman, as a person, I can't, because the system is stacked against me." She gestured toward herself, feeling even worse now than she'd felt moments earlier.

"So you're going to just give up? That doesn't seem like you, Suzanne. Can't remember you ever giving up on anything. They screwed you big time. This kind of thing happens more than people realize, and they continue to get away with it because of all the reasons you've just said. You have to understand, Suzanne, every change that's happened in civil, racial, and gender rights has come about only because someone had the guts to fight back and stand up and say no, they're not going to be screwed over. Don't let them walk all over you."

She just took in her sister, knowing she was dying to fight this. "Yes, but at what cost to their personal lives?" She shook her head and lifted her hands, because she still ached, thinking about how Toby could've done this to her. "Please, Karen, just drop it. Maybe I'll feel differently down the road, but right now…" She lowered her hands, resting them on the counter behind her, against which she was leaning.

"Okay, I won't push, but I will check back in. I seriously want you to think on it," Karen said. "Well, if you don't want to talk about letting me kick some serious ass and get you some well-entitled retribution, tell me, how are things for you and Harold?"

She took in her sister's interest. The fact was that she was still trying to figure out where she and Harold were, entirely. It wasn't as if they could just pick up where they left off, because they'd been kids, and now they weren't.

"We're good," she finally said.

Karen raised a brow. "Elaborate, please, Suzanne, because I remember you and Harold together in high school, how inseparable you were. I remember when things went south for you and how devastated you were. This isn't just casual and not really serious, like it was with Toby."

She knew her sister, just like the rest of her family, was wondering how serious she and Harold were—but then, so was she.

"Look, don't compare Harold and Toby, because the Toby thing was never going anywhere. I can see that now. As for Harold, well, he's here all the time. He's rented a nice condo in town. He has his place, and he's not worried about being seen with me. Would I like to bump it up to something more serious? Of course, but at the same time, he's not there yet, I think. I don't know."

What she did know was that he had a key to her house and had spent the previous night there, and the night before that, but the topic of what was next for them wasn't something she wanted to discuss with her family, considering she didn't know where Harold saw them. Maybe with dinner tonight, she could figure out what he was thinking.

Just then, she heard a car out front, and then the door opened.

"Hey, it's me! Whose fancy Mercedes is parked out front?" Harold called out before he stopped just outside the kitchen, wearing his deputy uniform, taking in her and her sister. She could see the open question in his amber eyes. "Karen, hey," he said as he stepped in and rested his hand on the refrigerator just above Suzanne's head, dragging his gaze from Karen back to her. "Did I walk in on something?"

"Just my sister trying to talk me into taking a chunk out of the chief, Toby, and his grandfather by suing the shit out of them."

Harold raised his brows.

"Don't worry," she said. "I told Karen no, because that

kind of thing is frowned upon, and I do want to be a fire-fighter again, although…"

"Hate to say this, Suzanne, but I think I'm going to side with Karen on this," Harold said.

For a second, she wasn't sure she'd heard him right, and she wondered if her expression showed how thrown she was. "Excuse me?"

Harold stepped in closer to her, his hand resting on the counter behind her. He was so close she could feel his heat. She was so damn comfortable around him, but she was still having trouble understanding where he was coming from.

"Look, babe, I know I said you'd basically be screwing yourself, and that's true, because of the system you're fight-ing, but the problem is that you're not getting your job back here anyway, because the chief, Toby, and his grand-father seem to wield all the power. The fire department shouldn't be controlled by individuals, but it is, so even if by some miracle Toby was no longer running the depart-ment, or Chief Burns retired, whoever is handpicked would already know that you caused a problem. You've already been painted with the scarlet letter, and those care-fully placed lies and insinuations will never go away. So yeah, sue them and make it hurt like hell, because as long as you live in Livingston, you'll never be a firefighter again."

What he was saying was something she didn't want to hear. "Fine, so I'll work the next county over," she said. "I already put my name in…"

He was shaking his head, and his expression had her pausing and looking over to Karen, who had also appar-ently figured out whatever this was.

"Okay, what the hell, you two?" Suzanne said. "What's going on?"

"So word's out, is it?" Karen said, crossing her arms over her chest, under her generous breasts.

Harold pulled in a breath and seemed to consider something. "When gossip starts, it turns into a runaway freight train. You've been labeled a problem, hard to work with. They say you don't have your team's back, aren't able to carry the load. An independent investigator was apparently hired, and he's already sided, off the record, with the department. Several of your team members have already come forward to say that the workplace stress is gone now with you not there, that they're not confident you can do your job in a fire, and they've sided with Toby's recommendation in having you fired. It's rumored that Kyle said you overstepped in challenging Toby and should've backed off, and a few said if they'd known you and the lieutenant were involved intimately, they'd have filed a complaint earlier."

She couldn't believe it. He hadn't pulled his gaze, and she knew he wasn't pulling any punches, either. That was something she'd loved about him, but at the same time, right now, she wished he wouldn't be quite so forthcoming.

Her chest ached, and for a minute she considered walking out so she could, what, lock herself in her tiny bathroom and cry? Then she felt his hand rubbing her arm, and he was right in front of her, both his hands on her.

She heard footsteps, then the front door, then a car outside as Karen left.

Harold was so close, and she knew he wasn't going to let her hide. She felt the tears burn, and when one slipped out, what did he do but kiss her? Her cheeks, both of them, and then her lips. His hands were now on her face, holding her with compassion.

"I'm sorry…" Her voice sounded raspy.

He was shaking his head. "No, don't you apologize. This isn't on you. Screw them."

She knew what he was saying. "So you want me to sue the department for killing my dream and for the fact that I'll never be a firefighter again?"

"I want you to get your pound of flesh," he said. "I'm sorry, Suzanne. You lost the battle, but you haven't lost the war. You just need to take a step back and come at it from a different direction. You know what? I'm here, and I have your back. At the same time, I think you need a distraction, so how about giving me a hand?"

He didn't give her space, and something about the way he touched her, even in all these small ways, had her feeling somewhat better.

"A hand in what?" she said. "This isn't some pity project you're tossing my way?"

His expression was comical, the way his lips hinted at a smile as he shook his head and lifted his hand. "Scout's honor, wouldn't do that. Besides, you heard there's a suspect in the fire."

She went to wipe a tear that had fallen, but Harold did that for her with his thumb, brushing it away. "Yes, I thought you arrested someone for it."

"We were ordered to arrest someone, but I'm thinking there's more to it. We have one surveillance video for one camera following one guy. But the thing is, as I pointed out to Marcus, we're missing surveillance from the other cameras in the store. I have the feeling that something about this is all wrong. I don't think our suspect did it, and if there's one thing I've learned, it's that if I have a feeling something isn't right, it usually isn't. So how about you tag along and be a second pair of eyes for me?"

"You mean detective work?"

He laughed softly. "In a way. I have hours of video to

watch, considering I've requested all the videos from all the cameras. I could use your help, because although the arson investigator's report gives the details of where the fire started, I'm thinking you may see something I won't."

She wasn't sure he was serious. She still thought he was tossing her crumbs.

He ran his hands over her arms again. "Come on, say yes."

She considered another second. "I still think this is a pity job."

"So that's a yes?" he said. There was something about Harold, how fun, encouraging, and teasing he was, that seemed to ease the ache she'd been breathing through.

"Sure," she said. "Why not?"

Chapter 18

His name was Joseph Rondin, seventeen, from the Blackfoot tribe. The boy was tall, six foot three, and lanky, wearing baggy jeans and a black ball cap. That was what Suzanne had seen of him as he was cuffed and walked in by Lonnie just after she'd shown up at the sheriff's office with Harold.

Now, Joseph was cuffed at Lonnie's desk across the room, and she could hear Lonnie and Marcus talking behind the closed door of his office. Of course, he didn't sound happy.

Harold said nothing as he brought up the video surveillance of Joseph. From Suzanne's perspective, it seemed the store cameras had zoomed in on him from the moment he walked through the door. That was the first video, the one that had originally been sent to the sheriff's office, the one the security guards and manager had stated showed who started the fire.

"So you're convinced it's not him based on what?" Suzanne asked Harold in a low voice as she stretched beside him where she sat, studying the computer screen.

"A hunch. If you look at the video they supplied, the only one, it's like they're handing this kid up on a platter. Some places would say, okay, good enough, but I don't see anything in there that tells me he started the fire."

She didn't think the kid could hear him. There was something about Joseph, a nervousness, and she realized she too would've looked a second or third time at him. Marcus's door opened, and he strode out, Lonnie behind him, still talking.

"Harold, you get through all that surveillance yet?" Marcus demanded. He had yet to say a word about her being there, helping out.

"Making my way through, but only just got the surveillance from the other cameras they omitted. I'm going to need more time."

Marcus stopped in front of Joseph, looking down at him, his hands resting on his duty belt. Lonnie walked around his desk, also looking down at him.

"So again, Joseph," Marcus said, "what were you doing in the store? Security says they've stopped you several times and had problems with you in the store—shoplifting, mischief, being a nuisance, up to no good…"

"They're lying," Joseph said. He was loud and sounded defensive. "I've never taken anything! Security is always hassling me every time I go in there. I never started that fire…"

"Then how do you explain the surveillance video?" Lonnie said, jumping in. "You looked nervous when you walked in the store, and even inside, you kept looking around as if checking whether someone was watching. How do you explain that?"

She knew Marcus had issues with Lonnie at times, and now was one of those time, as Lonnie had apparently arrested Joseph for arson after receiving a personal call from the mayor. She knew he'd gone over Marcus's head, considering Marcus had been stalling to give Harold time to go through all the surveillance video. That was what she'd learned in the forty minutes she'd been sitting there with Harold, watching a computer screen and seeing exactly what went on in her brother's stationhouse.

"Nervous!" Joseph said. "You're kidding, right? How the fuck am I supposed to act with everyone always watching me, expecting me to steal? Of course I'm nervous. You think I don't know I'm being watched? Then suddenly there's some security guy following me through the store or standing behind me, telling me I have to leave."

Suzanne couldn't pull her gaze from the boy. Marcus was looking down at him with that hard all-cop tough-love expression. She thought he was likely going to say something else to him, but he just shook his head and looked over to Harold before turning back to the suspect. Too many people already thought he did it.

"We're holding you on suspicion, that's all," Marcus said, then turned to Lonnie. "You're not charging him, because there isn't evidence yet. Just because the mayor and councillors want this closed, I'm not going to be pushed around, you got it? Cool your heels."

She could see Lonnie was ready to argue, but Marcus simply dragged his gaze away, back to the kid. He was tall, not someone she would've wanted to find herself caught alone in an alleyway with.

Harold said nothing, just watched as Joseph was uncuffed from the chair and taken into Marcus's office.

"You two, look faster," Marcus said. "The mayor is calling every five minutes, wanting to know why the suspect hasn't been charged yet. You got anything I can give him?" Her brother wasn't someone who could be pushed, but she'd heard the phone and expected someone to come through the door soon, demanding he do something.

"I'll have something when I have it, not before," Harold said. "Tell him that."

She wasn't sure, but she was positive a hint of a smile tugged at Marcus's lips. He said nothing else as he strode back into his office, only to poke his head out a second later and call out, "Charlotte, order a burger and soda from up the street for Joseph."

"Sure thing, Marcus," Charlotte said from where she sat behind her desk as the dispatcher. She was quiet, not the type of person Suzanne would have picked for Marcus, but at the same time, she was.

Marcus walked back into his office, and Charlotte was now on the phone. Lonnie, who seemed pissed, rummaged through a file and then picked up the phone, as well.

"So is this an average day of being a cop?" Suzanne said.

Harold was on his computer, pulling up more videos. He shook his head. There was something about his ability to focus, as if he wasn't going to be pulled into this pissing contest between Marcus and Lonnie.

"Nope, no such thing as an average day," he said. "Right now, this is about finding out who set the fire, who really set it, not who the store and the city want to be the fall guy. So get comfortable, because we could be at this awhile."

"So do we get popcorn, or is this part of a cop's job?" Suzanne said. She thought her eyes would go buggy from the hours of surveillance video they'd been watching on his computer and the number of people they'd seen go through the store and departments. Some she knew, but many she didn't.

She stood up from the chair he'd pulled over and stretched the kink in her back, never having sat so long before. Lonnie was long gone now. Joseph had been fed, and Suzanne's stomach had rumbled when she smelled the fast food delivery.

Harold was speeding up the video clip and then slowing it down, and he glanced away and up to her for only a second as she stepped behind him and rested her hands on his shoulders, which were impressive and hard. She tried to dig in and massage.

"Yeah, that's perfect," he said. "Just keep doing that for the next hour." He tapped the keyboard again. "It's not all action and glamor, being a cop. There's a lot of desk work and investigating that's boring and tedious. Then add in stakeouts, where nothing about them is exciting. Most times, looking for that needle in the haystack to do the job right requires attention to detail, and that means a ton of caffeine and doing your best not to fall asleep on the job— and there it is." He tapped the keyboard, and the video froze. He pointed at the screen. "Right there."

She leaned down, her hands still on his shoulders, and took in the still image of the surveillance, seeing the three screens for the toy department, clothing, and sporting goods.

"She's in every one of these. I thought it was odd, but look at her. She opens her purse. I couldn't tell what she was doing, but I think she lights a candle and then slides it under a stack of shirts. There's smoke a few minutes later with no one there. Same in sporting goods. She was over by the camping fuel and the matches, then again here, where the board games are. The arson investigator said it started in these three spots."

She took in what he was saying as he slowed down the video. She really had to look to see it. "You mean the woman who looks like a soccer mom…?"

He turned and looked up at her, leaning back in his chair, his hand on her. He was so close, and she loved being here with him as she took in what he was saying. There was something admirable about the way he'd demanded surveillance from all the cameras.

The woman seemed attractive, light hair, mid thirties, wearing what she thought were blue jeans and a nice shirt, carrying a basket of what looked like school supplies. Suzanne would never have picked her out, and she just stared again.

"Ah, okay, I see it—but I can't believe it."

He looked up at her and said nothing, then walked over to Marcus's office. The door was open, and he tapped on it, calling her brother.

"What do you have?" Marcus said.

As Suzanne stepped back, she realized that Charlotte was now gone, of course, being a mother to Eva. Harold and her brother were staring at the surveillance, the woman. She didn't know what to say.

"Any idea who that is?" Harold said. "She started each one."

From the way Marcus stared down, she knew he was uncomfortable. She didn't recognize the lady and wondered how hard it would be to find out who she was.

"Yeah, unfortunately. That's not good news," Marcus said, then winced and pulled in a breath as if considering what to do. "It's Cecilia Harding."

She wasn't sure she'd heard him right. "You're not talking about the Hardings who own the brewery…"

Harold glanced between them, so impartial.

Marcus had his thumb and forefinger on his chin,

rubbing. "Cecilia is married to Russell Harding, who owns the brewery, but Cecilia herself is a niece of Forest Chandler, the former fire chief. Yes, that would be Toby's grandfather. Cecilia's mother, I think her name was Jean, she died when Cecilia was, like, ten, remember?"

Suzanne was trying to put it together. She knew Toby came from a big family, with uncles, aunts, cousins. How many were there? Something about seeing this was so surreal, and it was hitting home in a way that was going to stir some major shit up.

"So how do you want to handle this?" Harold said. "I can pick her up."

Marcus was shaking his head, and she could see by his face that the political side of him was already thinking about how to come out ahead. "Nope, I'll do it. What I want you to do is save that video and call the DA while I pick up Cecilia." He allowed his gaze to drag over to her, then pulled his hand over his face. "Son of a bitch!" he muttered, then walked back into his office, where she could hear him say, "Okay, Joseph, it's your lucky day. You're officially cleared..."

She couldn't make out the rest.

Harold was already saving the videos, still looking at the screen.

"So how did you know to keep looking?" Suzanne said. "You know anyone else likely would've caved to the town council and charged that kid in there. It's not as if he has a clean record. He's been in trouble, right?"

Harold turned to her, giving her everything. "One of the things I learned at my time in Oklahoma City, in hate crimes, is that when a white person walks right in and takes something or does something, no one ever notices, because they're too busy looking at people like Joseph, people they assume are up to no good. Again, I've learned that when I get a feeling something isn't quite right, it generally isn't."

She took in her brother, who was walking Joseph out as the boy argued about his rights being violated, then glanced back to Harold, who was reaching for his keys. She realized now why her brother had hired him.

"My brother's lucky to have you," she said.

Harold pulled his keys from the drawer and gave her everything. "And you're not?" he said, stepping closer, sliding his hands around. He pulled her closer, and she knew there was no one else left in the office. She leaned in and pressed a kiss to his lips, letting it linger.

"Oh, I know I am," she teased. "So does this mean you're coming back to my place?"

He had somehow turned her and slid his hand around her waist, and he was now walking her to the door. "Well, yeah. Thought you'd cook me dinner and I'd help you figure out some what-nexts."

She looked up at him, seeing something teasing in those amber eyes. "What-nexts?"

He tapped her butt as he moved her out the door. "Yeah, you know, enough of this dancing around. How about we figure it out, my place or yours?"

She stopped outside, taking in something in his expression that she hadn't expected.

Then he said, "To live, of course. You think I want to keep switching keys every night? Let's figure it out. It's time, right?"

For a second, she didn't know what to say. Then she pulled in a breath. "Yeah, it's way past time."

The Commitment

THE O'CONNELLS

About The Commitment

As far as Marcus O'Connell is concerned, his situation is perfect. He's now living with the love of his life, Charlotte, and they're serving as guardians for Eva, a little girl he rescued whose mother is serving time in prison for a crime of which, in Marcus's mind, she was unfairly convicted.

But Charlotte isn't on board with Marcus's way of thinking. Because her divorce is now final, she wants—no, expects Marcus to want the same things she does. One of those things is a committed relationship, which, to Charlotte, means marriage. For Marcus, though, marriage is only a piece of paper, and it doesn't have anything to do with commitment.

However, when circumstances change for Eva, whom they both love deeply, Marcus is forced to make some hard decisions to keep both Eva and Charlotte, and he questions his reasons for not wanting marriage. What will he need to do to keep the child he and Charlotte now consider theirs?

Chapter 1

"You know my divorce is now final," Charlotte said as Marcus tucked his revolver in the gun safe on the top shelf of their small closet, which was packed with clothes. Charlotte's took up more than three quarters, so his meagre shirts were crammed in at one end.

He turned the dial of the safe and put his duty belt on the dresser, taking in Charlotte, who was in faded blue jeans and one of his old T-shirts, lingering in the doorway with a dishtowel over her shoulder. Her hair was hanging long and loose, and something about the way she was looking at him told him there was more.

"That's good, isn't it?" he said as he unbuttoned his uniform shirt and pulled it from his trousers before sitting on the queen-size bed that filled the master bedroom in their small older two-bedroom house, where it seemed as if everything they had was squeezed in. As he pulled off his shirt, he realized she hadn't responded from where she leaned in the doorway.

There was something about Charlotte. He swore the

woman could've made a grain sack look sexy, and yet, as he took her in, he could see she had something more on her mind.

"Charlotte…" he finally prompted.

She glanced over her shoulder into the narrow hallway before pulling in a breath and then giving him everything. "Well, of course, considering it took the full ninety days to clear a court even when my lawyer said it shouldn't take that long." She was holding up her bare hands now, fiddling with her fingers, as he leaned over and untied his tactical boots.

He slipped them off as he glanced up, waiting for her to finish. "Well," he said, "it's done now, so how long it took is kind of a moot point. Why don't you tell me what's really going on?"

She seemed to stiffen. The way she touched her ear, it was just one of the little things she did that told him she had something on her mind, something she was holding on to. He stood up and unbuckled his belt, and now she stepped into the bedroom and closed the door after glancing over her shoulder. He knew she was listening for Eva, who would likely be fast asleep, considering how late it was.

"How long have we been together now, Marcus—four months?" She crossed her arms, and all that did was accentuate her remarkable bust.

"About that."

She nodded, but it seemed he still hadn't figured out where this was going. "Well, it has been that long, add in a day or two, since we got Eva. We're a family, we're settled, and I guess I expected you'd have made things more permanent, considering I'm no longer married to Jimmy Roy. I took back my maiden name. Had to, with the state law and all, which is bringing all sorts of complications, considering all my legal documents and licenses have my married name."

He pulled in another breath, wishing she'd just say everything she was thinking. He felt as if he were walking a tightrope. "I would say this is permanent," he said. "We're living together, looking after Eva. We're a family…"

She was nodding, and it was then that he realized what she was expecting. "In every way that matters," she said, "but I kind of expected you to ask me to marry you, to make it official, you and me, Mr. and Mrs. O'Connell. I thought that's where we were going. I mean, I've loved you for so long, I just never figured we wouldn't already be married by now."

Marriage…so she wanted something official, on paper, a ring on her finger. Why was it that he was hesitating?

"Is this what you want, Charlotte?"

There it was, the way she could suddenly turn on a dime: the annoyance, the passion, the emotions that could have her becoming unreasonable. Every part of her seemed to stiffen as if she were getting ready to stand her ground on a topic he wasn't entirely sure how he felt about.

"Seriously, Marcus? I want you to want it. Now I'm starting to think that maybe I'm the one who's been misreading things. Of course I want it all, marriage, family, a life with you, but not if you don't. Just forget I said anything."

He caught the edge of her temper as she rested her hand on the doorknob, ready to turn it and walk out. He pressed his hand over her head to the door, holding it shut.

"Don't walk away all pissed and angry," he said. "I asked a simple question, Charlotte. I'm not a mind reader. It's been a long day."

She turned and pressed her back against the door, and she was so close that he was touching her. Having her there, he couldn't imagine going back to how he'd lived before, single and alone.

"Maybe not, Marcus, but right now you're making me feel as if this is it, that I shouldn't want anything more, that living together is all the permanence you need or want. I guess I just feel that…" She shrugged and looked away, pressing her teeth into her lower lip.

"You feel what? Come on, Charlotte. This works only if you share everything. It's been a long day, I'm tired, and you think I've been ignoring you. Of course everything is good, and maybe I just never thought that getting married would make a difference. I love you, you know that, so what would be different if we were married? It's just a piece of paper…"

"One that would tie us together, Marcus. It would be official. I know everyone thinks and believes that because we're living together and have Eva, we're married, but the thing is that it matters. It matters to me, and I know it matters to you, considering that during all the years I stayed married to Jimmy Roy because neither of us was willing to give up the house, you wouldn't allow yourself to become involved with me. As you said, separated is still married. Don't bullshit me, Marcus, because I know marriage does mean something to you."

He pushed away from the door. "Of course it means something. While you were married to him, you and I couldn't be together, because married is married. Now you're not, so I guess you are right about that much. It does matter…"

The fact was that Karen was the only one of his siblings who was married. What was it about his siblings, how they were different with each other than with everyone else? Something had bound their family together, yet when their father had walked out on all of them, it had destroyed Marcus's idea of family and commitment.

He stepped back, brushing the bed, wanting to strip out of his pants and climb into a hot shower and try to forget the pile of paperwork waiting for him at the sheriff's office. Charlotte was silently waiting for him to make a move, to say something, when all he wanted was for her not to have brought it up.

"I don't know what you want me to say, Charlotte. I love you, and I love Eva and what we have, but at the same time, I'm not sure a piece of paper is going to make a difference for me. Maybe I'll feel different down the road, but right now…"

She pressed her hand over the flat of his chest, and he could see it in the way she looked at him and forced a smile to her lips. She gave her head a toss. There wasn't a chance she could hide the hurt that he'd never wanted to put there.

"It's okay, Marcus. Forget I said anything," she said. Then she stepped back and pulled open the door.

"That's the thing, Charlotte. You and I both know you can't un-say something, and you and I can't forget it."

She pressed her hand to the doorframe as she stepped out and glanced back to him. "You're right, but I guess I have my answer. I'll heat up the leftover dinner for you. You have to be hungry."

Instead of waiting for him to say something, she walked away, her footsteps squeaking on the floorboards of the old house. All Marcus could do as he pulled in another breath, wanting to kick his own ass, was realize that instead of resolving anything, their discussion had revealed something about his relationship with Charlotte, which he'd thought was perfect. Now, it simmered with an underlying tension, all because she wanted to get married and he didn't.

Chapter 2

"So what's going on with you and Charlotte?" Ryan said as he rested two cases of beer, stout and amber ale, on the already full island in their mom's kitchen, then pulled open the fridge and shoved them all in.

"What are you talking about?" Marcus said. He lifted his gaze to the window over the sink, which looked out into the backyard, where Charlotte was sitting at the patio table. Eva was perched on her knee, and his mom, Suzanne, and Karen were sitting and talking with her.

"Oh, come on. While you're in here, making burgers for everyone, alone—and where's Owen, by the way? He usually has the grill fired up and ready, but his van isn't outside."

"No idea. Expected him to be here already. Mom said he had a call, some plumbing emergency, but he should be here soon…" He trailed off as the door opened and both Harold and Jack strode into the kitchen from where they'd also been out back.

"Heard the beer is here," Harold said. "Suzanne's put

in her order." He was still in his deputy uniform, whereas Jack was in dark dress pants and a light blue dress shirt with the sleeves rolled up, his dark hair short and neat. Everything about him still had Marcus watching him closely from afar. Although Karen seemed happy, he had his doubts on their so-called marriage and how there could be a happily ever after considering everything that had happened between them.

Ryan handed a stout to Harold and held one out to Jack, who just shook his head. Right. Another thing about the man was that he seemed to sit on the sidelines with water instead of alcohol.

Marcus realized Ryan was still waiting for him to say something as he set one of the amber ales on the counter in front of him. Marcus tossed the last burger patty on a cookie sheet with the other dozen he'd already made and then set the bowl in the sink and washed his hands, taking in the way Ryan glanced out the window to where Charlotte sat with her back to him.

"She's fine," Marcus finally said. "Everything's fine between us. Not sure what you're getting at." He wiped his hands, lifted the beer, and took a swallow, watching as Harold and Jack realized they'd obviously walked in on something.

"That's not what Jenny said," Ryan replied.

Marcus dragged his gaze over to him. His brother was still in his park uniform. It seemed Marcus was the only one who'd gone home after work and changed into blue jeans and a faded shirt.

"What, exactly, did Jenny say?" he asked. "And where, exactly, are Jenny and Alison tonight, anyway?"

There it was, an exchange between Jack and Ryan. Evidently, Karen's husband knew something, too. Harold was the only one who hadn't pulled his gaze from Marcus, and he wasn't sure what he was thinking or what he knew, considering he was hard to read.

"Jenny and Alison stopped at the store to get burger buns and are picking up dessert, too. They should be here soon," Ryan said. "You do realize all the girls talk—Karen, Suzanne, Jenny, Charlotte. And Mom knows everything, as she seems to always be there, hearing about us."

Marcus dragged his gaze over to Ryan and then took in both Harold and Jack.

"They seem to share everything," Jack said, jumping in. "I learned that from Karen."

There was something about this that didn't sit right with Marcus. At the same time, he knew how frosty his relationship had become since Charlotte had brought up the fact that she was waiting for him to slip a ring on her finger.

"Look, her divorce is only just final," Marcus said. "I don't understand what it's about, this need to have it all so formal and so fast. What's the difference, really, between a piece of paper and how things are now? I'm committed, we're a family, we live together…"

Ryan seemed to hesitate, and from the expression on Harold's face and the way Jack didn't pull his gaze from him, Marcus realized that maybe they weren't on the same page.

"Excuse me, are we talking…?" Ryan gestured with his beer as he lifted a brow.

"Marriage," Marcus said. "Charlotte wants to get married, and I'm guessing that's not what you heard, so I have to wonder what it is that you're talking about."

All his brother did was shake his head, and Marcus wondered what wasn't being said.

"Ah, well, that makes sense, then," Ryan said, then actually glanced over to Jack, who only shook his head.

Again, Marcus wasn't sure what to make of their expressions. Meanwhile, Harold was taking them all in as if waiting until he'd heard everything to add what he did or didn't know.

"You want to elaborate, then?" Marcus said. "Because I'm still not sure why she's so insistent of the formality, considering how things didn't work out so well for her in her first marriage. I didn't know she was sharing everything about us. Not sure how I feel about that."

"They all talk about us," Ryan said. "Thought you knew that. Jenny said something about you having commitment issues."

He wasn't sure if his eyes bugged out. "Excuse me?" he said. He found himself turning and taking in the sight through the window, wondering what Charlotte was saying to his mom. Add in Suzanne and Karen, and they all seemed so deep in conversation. "I don't have commitment issues. If I did, I'd still be living the single life in my bachelor pad without Charlotte or Eva. I have an instant family now. Just because we haven't officially tied the knot, with her taking my name so she can tell everyone she's my wife, and vice versa, doesn't mean I'm not committed."

"So what's holding you back?" Jack said, crossing his arms over his chest.

Marcus wasn't sure how he felt about his brother-in-law questioning him this way, adding his opinions on anything he did with his life. "Nothing's holding me back. I just don't understand why she's making such a big deal about this." In fact, just talking about marriage had him feeling things he wasn't entirely comfortable with.

"Well, it is a big deal, apparently, for Charlotte," Ryan said. "Some women want marriage, and evidently, Charlotte thinks you're not all in, is what Jenny said."

Marcus dragged his gaze from Ryan over to Jack and

Harold, who still had said nothing, which had Marcus wondering exactly where he stood in the equation with Suzanne. Were they living at his place, her place? All he knew was that they seemed to be together, but at the same time, there'd been no mention of where their future was headed.

"That's ridiculous," Marcus said. "So does Jenny agree with her? I mean, you two aren't married, but you live together, and then there's Alison. You're her father. You're a family. So are you and Jenny getting married anytime soon? If we're talking commitment issues…"

From the way Ryan shook his head and the face he made, Marcus could see he'd hit a nerve. "I've asked Jenny, and she said no for now. She's happy with the way things are. Don't try to spin this my way, Marcus. At the same time, considering how things went down with Wren, can you blame her? She's asked me to give her time. She may warm up to the idea down the road, but right now, all she wants is to maintain the status quo. I've pushed all I can. I sold my house and live in hers, but I can see the moment she feels cornered and panics. I'll give her that. I'm not pushing. Charlotte wants something different, evidently. Apparently, she wants forever with you, a permanent ring, signed papers, the whole deal. So if you're all in, why not get married? Or is there something going on, and maybe Charlotte's right that you're not really feeling the need to get married and head in that direction?"

How had they ever gotten on this topic? Right, so the women all talked. Great. He wondered what else they knew of the personal things that went on between him and Charlotte. Likely, he needed to have a word with her about how much she was sharing.

"Now you're putting words in my mouth," Marcus said, "and you know what? This is really something that should be between me and Charlotte, something we should work out and discuss and decide."

Yes, he'd sit Charlotte down and find out what else she'd decided to share with his family. He wasn't the bad guy here.

Then he heard the front door open, bringing in the voices of Jenny, Alison, and Owen.

"You're right," Jack said. "It is between you two—but you should know that Karen happens to be on your side in the matter."

Just then, Jenny walked in, carrying a brown paper bag with buns, followed by Alison, who rested a pie on the counter. Owen stepped around her and pulled open the fridge door to take out a beer.

"Anyone start the grill?" was all Owen said as he twisted the cap off one of the amber ales, looking grungy in a faded shirt and jeans with tears in the knees. He started to the back door, taking them all in, and Marcus realized something was off about his brother.

"Just waiting on you," he said. "Burgers are ready to go as soon as you are…"

That was all he managed to get out, as Owen kept walking out the door. He said something to the women, then walked over to the barbecue.

Marcus gestured outside toward him. "What was that about?"

All Ryan did was shake his head before leaning down and kissing Jenny.

"He's got girl trouble," Alison said, jumping in. Marcus took in his precocious teenage niece, who still had a chip on her shoulder.

Ryan stepped around her, rested his hand on her shoulder-length hair, and rustled it. "You know something we don't?"

Even Jenny was giving everything to Alison, who shrugged. For a minute, he didn't think she would add anything more. Her prickly teenage attitude could drive them all crazy.

"If you know something, spill," Ryan finally said, and what did she do but roll her eyes at him?

"Maybe I saw something." She took them in and let it linger for added dramatic effect before rolling her eyes again. "The diner he stops in every day for lunch. I saw him with a waitress who works there."

Marcus found himself leaning in. "And...?" he finally said.

"Well, seems they're in an on-again, off-again relationship. Today they got into it. I heard her say she was done, telling him to pick up his things since he can't get off the fence and commit one way or another. They were fighting out behind the diner in the alley. She walked away, and then he walked away. There you go: girl trouble." She shrugged as if that answered everything.

At least they weren't talking about him and Charlotte anymore. Alison then walked out back, and they all seemed to glance out toward Owen, who was now cleaning the grill alone. If Marcus considered it, he looked as if he were brooding.

"Did you know?" Ryan said to Jenny, who was shaking her head.

"No. There's one thing about Owen that sets him apart from all of you O'Connells. He's a closed book. As much as you all have your little secrets, with Owen there, if he doesn't want you to know, he can hold on to something way better than any of you, so much so that you wouldn't even know he was hiding anything in the first place. And that's saying something, considering you O'Connells are about the most difficult and secretive bunch I've ever met."

At the way Jenny said it, he didn't miss the hint of amusement that tugged at Harold's lips. Even Jack seemed to agree. He took in Ryan, who slid his arms around Jenny, pulling her back against him.

"That's ridiculous," Ryan said.

Jenny let her gaze land on Marcus before dragging it over to Harold and Jack. "No, it's not. Pretty sure you two can back me up."

Harold lifted the beer, which Marcus knew was for his sister. "You know, that's my cue to leave and get this beer out to Suzanne."

For a minute, he thought Jack was going to say something, but he changed his mind. "I think I'll join you," he said, then followed Harold out.

That just left Ryan, Jenny, and Marcus.

"Cowards," she muttered under her breath, still leaning against Ryan, who seemed content to keep her there as he kissed her cheek. She let her gaze linger before dragging it back over to Marcus. "So much for the other halves sticking together."

She patted Ryan's arm as she stepped out of his embrace. Then she too went out back. He could hear the family talking, laughing, but he didn't know what they were saying.

Ryan reached for his beer and then gestured with his chin. "Looks like Owen's ready for the burgers. If I were you, I'd figure out this marriage thing with Charlotte. If you don't want it, just make sure she understands, but most of all, figure out in your own mind what you do want. Because if Jenny is wondering, that means Suzanne and Karen are too—and then there's Mom."

Great point. As he turned his head and glanced out the back window, he realized his mom was watching them. So what did he do but pick up the tray of raw burger patties and start to the back door?

He pressed his hand on it, about to step out, when Ryan said, "You know, as long as I've known you, Marcus, I've never seen you into another woman like you are Charlotte. Even I knew, for you, she was always the one. Is this really about not wanting to get married, or is there something else that has you thinking maybe she isn't the one?"

Instead of answering a question he didn't have an answer for, he pushed open the screen door. Before stepping out, he turned back to his brother and said, "Bring another beer out for me when you come."

Then he emerged onto the patio. Everyone had been talking, but just as quickly, they all looked over and up to him, and everyone was quiet.

Chapter 3

"**A**re you still taking me to see my mom tomorrow, Marcus?" Eva said. She was on the bottom bunk, and he pulled up the ladybug quilt, a gift from his mom. The matching sheets were from Karen, and the two teddy bears she slept with were from Jenny and Alison. Suzanne, he knew, was responsible for the light pink walls. There was something about this room, completely stamped with the personality of this little girl who'd stolen his heart.

"I told you I would. We'll leave first thing in the morning. Do you want to talk about seeing your mom and where she is in jail?"

The fact was that each time he'd taken Eva to see her mother in prison, he'd had to carry her out as they left, her crying into his shoulder. It was a place filled with despair, anger, and nothing that would have her sleeping peacefully at night. He hated how it affected her, but at the same time, not seeing her mother would've been that much worse.

He knew Charlotte wished he'd consider not taking her, but seeing her daughter gave Reine hope that there was someone on the outside who loved her and was waiting for her. However, as he watched the little girl that he and Charlotte had taken in, Marcus couldn't imagine a time when she wouldn't be with them.

"Is she okay?" Eva said. "Mommy looks so sad every time we see her. I don't like her having to stay there in jail. How come I can't hug her? And the scary police there, they yelled at Mommy. They scare me…"

He could see her fear. How could he explain the cruelty of a system that stripped away every right a person had? "Well, Eva, we talked about this. There are rules in prison. Your mom can hug you only once before the visit and once after. She has to sit across the table, and those police are guards. They're there to make sure everyone follows the rules. Of course she's sad because she doesn't get to live with you, but I do know your mom is happy that you're here with me and Charlotte and that we're looking after you. She cries because she's so happy to see you."

Every Saturday morning, they took Eva to see Reine. Something about taking her into that place made him wish she'd never have to experience it again, but at the same time, this was what he did as a sheriff, putting people away. Except Reine was someone he'd never have arrested if he'd had the power not to. Everything about her situation had been out of his hands.

He sat at the edge of the bed, tucking in this sweet little girl who'd seen too much fear and heartache, far too much, more than a six-year-old should have experienced.

"But we didn't see Mommy last week," she said. "They wouldn't let us see her. How come, Marcus? I want to see her."

What was he supposed to say? Reine had been put in solitary for reasons he still didn't know, and finding out once they'd got there had been the worst thing for Eva. He couldn't explain it to her, and the warden still hadn't called him back after the three messages he'd left. It was a side of the system he'd never had to face, cruel and uninformed, leaving him not knowing what was happening inside to a woman who'd only experienced the worst side of life.

"I wish I could tell you, Eva. I wish you didn't have to see your mommy in that place. But you know I'll be there with you, and so will Charlotte. We won't let anything happen to you. I know it's loud and scary, and your mommy has to sleep there, but it won't be forever. I just need you to be strong, and you know you can talk to me and Charlotte about it, and if there's ever a time you don't want to go, you just say so."

She just nodded. He wished he didn't have to take her, but at the same, he couldn't not. Reine was her mother, and as bad a place as it was, she still needed to see her.

"You promise I'll see her tomorrow?" Eva said.

He just took in the innocence and how sweet she was. "I promise you I'll do my very best to make sure you see her," he said. He knew that was all he could do. Even being a sheriff didn't give him any say in the prison. It was an entirely different system, with different rules, the kind of place that bred a different way of life. He didn't know how anyone could come out of there rehabilitated and not permanently scarred and damaged.

"Okay, go to sleep," Marcus said. "Do you want me to put the nightlight on?" He stood up, touching the Tinkerbell lamp that Luke had given Eva, which was on the white dresser Owen had bought and put together for her. Everything in this room was for Eva, from his family—her family.

"Yes, and can you leave the door open?" she said.

Of course he would. He picked up the nightlight and plugged it into the outlet before turning off the lamp.

"How's that?"

"Did you lock the window?" she said.

He rested his hand on it, seeing that the latch was set and it was locked.

"Up tight," he said. "You know I'm going to keep you safe. We're right next door, and we can hear you. I'll check on you again before I go to bed."

He hoped she'd sleep through the night tonight. He never knew when she'd have a bad dream.

She nodded again. "Goodnight, Marcus."

He stopped in the doorway, seeing her watching him. "Goodnight, sweet pea," he said.

Then he started down the hall and into their bedroom, seeing Charlotte sitting on the bed in a T-shirt and pajama shorts, brushing out her hair, damp from the shower. She flicked her hazel eyes up to him, and there was something there, a hesitation, before she said, "Eva all settled in?"

He nodded as he leaned in the doorway, taking in this woman he loved, her round face. Everything about her was passionate and kind. She gave everything to Eva, to him, and he couldn't imagine being without them. Everything he had now was exactly what he wanted, yet he didn't know if he could give her what *she* wanted.

"She's asking about seeing Reine tomorrow, about whether she's going to be able to see her. I know she's worried the same thing will happen this week and she won't get to."

Charlotte let out a sigh and rested her brush on the bed. "The warden still hasn't called you back?"

He shook his head. "Only thing I was able to find out was some ridiculous write-up for behavior, which could mean anything. Maybe she talked back to a guard, looked at someone the wrong way, said the wrong thing, or none of the above…" He'd already been warned off once by the warden, who'd told him that his interference wouldn't be tolerated.

"So we don't know if we'll be able to see Reine," Charlotte said. "Marcus, I don't want to put Eva through that. She cried all the way home. She was heartbroken, not being able to see her mom. Maybe until we know for sure, we shouldn't go…"

Marcus stepped into the room and up to the bed, shaking his head. "No, Charlotte. What would we say to her? She needs to see her mother. She wants to see her. Us keeping her here and saying no to a visit would be worse. I'm not going to tell her no. I'll call again first thing in the morning before we go…"

"And if we get there and we can't see her, then what?" she said, cutting him off, and he didn't miss the edge in her tone.

"The truth, that at least we tried. That's all we can do, Charlotte—but why don't we talk now about the fact that you seem to think I have commitment issues, or is that not what you told Jenny?"

She glanced away and seemed to hesitate as she tapped the brush on the bed, then rested it on the bedside table. He wondered if she was trying to figure out what to say. Then she lifted her gaze to him. "I'm sorry, Marcus, but don't you?"

There it was, getting right to the point.

"If I did, we wouldn't be living together," he said. "I guess I don't understand why you went to Jenny. And, for that matter, what is this about you, my sisters, my mom, and Jenny all sharing all kinds of personal stuff? I'm not sure how I feel about that, Charlotte, having everyone knowing what's going on between us. It's private, you and me…"

"I didn't share anything personal," she said. "Jenny

asked me what was wrong. She knew my divorce was final, and so did your sisters and your mom. We were talking a few weeks back, and Karen had said something about how long it was taking for the judge to clear divorce decrees through his court, longer than usual. Then Suzanne asked when you and I were planning on getting married now that it was final. I said we hadn't really talked about it. I guess that planted a seed in my mind, so then when you said nothing, it bothered me. Bringing it up last night, I never expected the response I got. I guess when I saw Jenny today, she knew something was wrong, so I told her I brought up marriage and you shot it down. Is it that you don't want me talking to anyone about how I feel? I don't see how that's personal or private…" She shrugged.

He was still stuck on what she'd said, the fact that she'd been thinking about it for so long. "I didn't shoot you down, Charlotte. I said I'm happy with how things are right now with you and me and Eva. I still don't know how a piece of paper changes anything."

She lifted her chin, then pulled the covers back and slid under the sheets. "Marcus, if that isn't commitment issues, I don't know what is. It's fine, as I said. Yes, I'm bothered, but let's just go to bed. You want to leave things as they are? Consider them left."

Then she lay down on her side, giving him her back, and she reached over and flicked off her bedside lamp, leaving just the soft hall light.

It seemed that for Charlotte, forgetting about this was exactly what wasn't going to happen.

Chapter 4

It was always the same, the hour and a half spent driving to the women's prison, the sense of urgency and restlessness. They left after breakfast. Eva had already changed outfits twice. She had been up at five, and he was sure she hadn't slept well. She sat in the back seat of the Subaru for the relatively easy drive. He knew she was on edge, but at least she'd stopped asking if she'd get to see her mom.

Marcus still hadn't received a call back from the warden. He wasn't sure what was up with her and why she was being so obstinate. He was sure she was sending him a message so he understood that he had no say in how she ran things.

He glanced over to Charlotte, who'd said nothing to him other than to ask whether he wanted eggs and to give him his coffee. In fact, she'd feigned sleep the night before when he climbed into bed and tried to pull her closer. He wasn't liking how frigid and icy things had turned. But now wasn't the time to get into it.

He also realized, as he drove, that Charlotte needed

something more than his words, his pleas to give him time to figure out where he was. Marcus didn't have commitment issues, and even thinking it now had him glancing back to Eva, whose only worries and angst were about wanting to see her mother. Charlotte was staring straight ahead, sunglasses on, and not once had she looked his way. Right, the wall was up.

He pulled into the parking lot of the prison, which was almost full, and spotted the lineup to go in. He wondered how many of the faces would be the same ones he saw every week. A few of the faces behind bars were those of women he'd been responsible for putting there.

He turned off the engine and flicked his gaze to the rear-view mirror just as Eva unbuckled her seatbelt. He glanced over to Charlotte and reached over to her, touching her arm, taking in her light blue blouse, blue jeans, and hoodie. She turned her head but didn't take her sunglasses off.

"We'll talk later," he said.

"About?" she replied. Boy, the woman could hold on to things.

He slid his hand down her arm and settled it on the back of her hand, feeling her trying to fight the way she wanted him. She was tense, but he didn't pull away. "I think you know," he said. "You shut me out, but that's not the way to handle this. I love you. I think you know that."

"Marcus, can we go in? I want to see Mommy." Eva stood up in the back, touching his seat.

He turned his head to her. "Yes, let's go."

When Charlotte didn't say anything, he patted her hand twice and climbed out after tucking his sunglasses in the center console. He pulled open Eva's back door, and she hopped out. Charlotte walked around the front of the car, taking in the prison, the people lined up. Her sunglasses were now gone, and her gaze couldn't hide anything from him.

He held Eva's hand as he started walking, and Charlotte fell in beside him and slipped her hand into his other hand, leaning against him with a gentle nudge.

"I know you do," was all she said.

They lined up and waited their turn. He looked to Eva, who hadn't let go of his hand, and then over to Charlotte, who lingered beside him, touching him.

She looked up to him. "You know I just want it all with you," she added, then let out a breath, because there was just something about the way she said it, the way she was touching him. She really was all in with him, so why wasn't he down on one knee, asking her to be his, officially, permanently, forever?

He gave his head a shake and looked up to the sky, seeing the clouds. Instead of saying anything, he just squeezed Charlotte's hand.

It was their turn. As they passed the guards, he worried for a moment about being told there would be no visitors for Reine, but they made it into the visiting area and sat at a table, and Charlotte was now sitting in a chair with Eva on her lap. He didn't know what she was saying, but he knew she was trying to ease some of Eva's fears.

Marcus took in the guards, a few of the inmates that he'd personally arrested, and then he saw her. Reine was being led in. Her face had a red mark, a bruise. Her dark hair was tied back, and her prison garb was unflattering. She walked right over and called Eva, who jumped from Charlotte's lap and ran to her mom and hugged her. All Marcus could do was take in the guards, who he knew would step in if it went too far.

Reine squatted down and hugged Eva, lifting her hazel eyes to meet Marcus's, and he took in the fear and sadness and something else that he hadn't seen before. Then she reached up and pulled at Eva's arms, which were around her neck.

"Come on, Eva," she said. "Sit down and tell me everything you did this week. You look so happy, so pretty."

Charlotte hugged Reine before she sat across the table from them, and Marcus rested his hand on her shoulder. It was all he could offer. He took a seat, Eva sitting between him and Charlotte, and just listened to the back and forth of mother and daughter as Eva talked nonstop about his family, her cousin Alison, and everything that had gone on with them over the past few weeks.

He tuned out what they were saying, wondering what had happened to Reine to leave such a bruise on her face. There was just something about the guards watching and the other inmates there. Everything seemed so unsettled. Maybe it had always been, but it seemed there was something more.

"What happened?" he finally said to Reine, knowing their two hours were almost up. He gestured to his face.

She shrugged and kept her hands linked together on the table in front of her. "I slipped, is all. It's nothing. I was just clumsy." She pulled her gaze from him.

He knew it wasn't true and wondered if it had anything to do with her being in solitary.

"Eva, you know I love you very much," Reine said. "Visiting hours are almost over, so I want to talk to Marcus alone. Would you mind staying a bit?" She pulled her gaze from Eva and gave everything to him. He knew there was something she didn't want to share in front of her daughter.

"No, Mommy! I don't want to go yet…"

"Hey, Eva, we're going to come back," Marcus said, "but I want to have a talk with your mom, okay? It's going to be okay." He glanced to Charlotte, who he knew understood. That was just another thing he loved about her.

"Hey, Eva, come on, it's okay," she said. "Marcus just needs to make sure your mom is okay. Let them talk. We'll see her again."

He wasn't sure how she did it, but Charlotte somehow managed to get Eva up, and Marcus gestured to the guard, because as Reine was hugging her daughter, the woman strode over.

"Her daughter's leaving," Marcus said. "She's just saying goodbye." He didn't want a repeat incident or to have to worry she'd be written up.

The guard must have understood, as her dark eyes lingered for a second before she nodded.

Reine held Eva tight, and she swiped at a tear that slipped out. When she pushed her daughter away, he could see that it had taken everything in her, considering that was the kind of love someone couldn't hide. "You go on now," she said, "and remember I love you. Be a good girl this week for Marcus and Charlotte."

Marcus just watched as Charlotte held Eva's hand and they walked to the door, to the guard, and left. When he turned back to Reine, he could see she was having a hard time. She sat back down, wiping her tears and sniffling, but she quickly pulled it together and blew out a breath, long and loud.

Marcus sat across from her and took in her face, the face of a woman who, in his mind, didn't belong here. "So are you going to tell me what happened to your face? We both know you didn't fall. Last week when we came, you were in solitary. What happened?"

She lifted her gaze, and he wasn't sure he liked what he saw. "I never thought I'd have to watch my back every waking hour in here. It seems my daughter living with a cop, one who put a few in here, has put a target on me. Doesn't matter who did this. Nothing will happen. Solitary…what can I say? I never saw it coming. It's so easy for someone who has it out for you to say you did something when you didn't."

"I can talk to the warden," he started, but she was shaking her head.

"No, please don't, because that would only make it worse. You think she doesn't know what goes on in her prison? Of course she does, and so do the guards. It seems I was the only one who didn't. Who could have ever figured I'd be trading one way of survival out there for another in here? I'll be fine," she added, then glanced over her shoulder. He wondered which of the inmates or guards she was terrified of.

"Keep your head down," he said. "Don't make waves. So which one is causing you some heat? Is it someone I put away?" he asked, hoping she'd tell him. But at the same time, even if she did, what could he do from the outside? Nothing.

"A few of them," she said. "It only adds fuel to the fire when you come here with Eva. They know my daughter is living with a cop, one who's responsible for them being here. Didn't expect it, but at the same time, Eva seems happy. I'm glad for that." She clasped her hands tightly, doing her best to keep it together. "You said you would look after her, and you have."

"I promised you. She is looked after, and we care very much that she's okay. She misses you, though."

She lifted her gaze, and he locked on to the hardness he'd seen from her only one time. "I can see you care for my daughter, you and Charlotte—but I need to know if you love her." She didn't pull her gaze from his.

"Yeah," he said. "She's found a way into my heart, and

Charlotte's, and my family's, too. How could we not? She's part of our family now."

Reine only nodded and pulled in another breath. "Then this will make it easier. I don't want you to bring her here again."

He wasn't sure he'd heard her correctly. "What? No, I can't do that. She needs to see you. As hard as this is, it's important for Eva…"

But Reine was shaking her head, so damn determined. "No, you listen to me. She can't come anymore. If she does, I'll turn you away, all of you. This time here is difficult and damn hard, but I can do it if I know she's loved and looked after, and I see that. I mean, even when I get out of here in how many years, then what? No. You said you would take her, and I gave you guardianship of her. I signed away my rights. Would you give them back when I get out and let Eva go?

"And then what? If anything, I've had a rude awakening. What she has with you, I'm not going to be able to give that to her. Where would I take her? I don't know. It would be hard. All I can remember since Eva was a baby has been hardship and stress. Yes, I love her, but when I see her now, I don't want her coming into this place anymore. You'll keep Eva?"

The way she said it, he knew something had happened in here, and it was making her do the one thing he'd never expected her to do, give up her daughter.

"Of course we'll keep Eva. We've never talked about when you get out, but we'll work it out, Reine. You're still her mother. What you're talking about now is never seeing her again, and I know Eva wouldn't be okay with that. What about your father? I know you've heard from him."

He heard the guards announce the end of visiting

hours, but he needed more time. Reine stood up. Around them, he could hear other inmates saying goodbye.

"Yes, I've seen my dad," she said. "Maybe that's why I'm doing this. In his way, he loves me, but he has a life somewhere else. He asked to take Eva, and I considered it…but after what happened to drive us apart, even though I'm sure he'd do his best for Eva, I don't want that for her. After I get out, she'll be how old? She'll be loved, settled, with a life. I can't yank her from that."

"Reine, listen to me. Don't do this. We'll figure something out. Don't give up…"

She was shaking her head as she stood before him. "Just let me know how she's doing. Send me photos. But I'm serious, Marcus: Don't come back here again. Don't bring Eva with you, because you'll be taken off my visitation list. Tell me now that you'll keep Eva. I gave you guardianship. I've signed away my rights. Will you and Charlotte take her, adopt her? Please…"

It would be too easy to say yes.

"You'll regret it one day if we do," he said, "and she'll hate you and be angry because she can't see you."

The guard was coming their way. Everyone was leaving, and she had to go, and so did he—but he still had so much to say to her.

"Maybe so, Marcus, but I need to know you won't abandon her." She lifted her gaze just as the guard drew closer. He could see the panic, the way she was getting ready to fight if he didn't say what she needed to hear.

"I'd never abandon her," he said. "Of course we'll keep her, but it doesn't have to be this permanent."

Reine turned and started walking to the open door that led to the cell block, the one the other prisoners had already gone through, but she glanced back to him. "Yes, it does," she said. "Because I love her so much, I can give her up to you and Charlotte. Keep her happy."

Then she was gone, and he was the only one left. He took in the guard and his open door, and he started walking. He didn't have a clue how he'd get Eva to understand.

Chapter 5

"So this is where you're hiding out," Karen said as she strode out the front door of Ryan and Jenny's house to join him on the porch, where he sat in the dark alone. "Charlotte's filling everyone in on what happened."

The streetlights were on, and he could hear the sounds of his family, of everyone inside the house. Karen wore a blue and white cotton dress with a white sweater pulled overtop, her legs and feet bare. Her hair was pulled up in a messy bun, and she was holding a glass of white wine as she sat in one of the porch chairs beside him.

"You know, it may not be a bad thing..." she started. Maybe the dark look he gave her was why she stopped talking and let out a sigh.

"And how's that?" he said. "Reine got a fucked-up deal, and now she wants to give her kid away." He knew that wasn't the way of it, but at the same time, he didn't have a clue what he was going to say to Eva. It would crush her, hearing that she couldn't see Reine again. "Maybe in a few weeks, she'll change her mind. Let's hope she does."

His sister didn't say anything for a second, just lifted

her glass and took a swallow of wine. His let his gaze linger on the glass, wondering how many she'd had—two, maybe three.

"So is Jack okay with you finishing that wine?" he said. "Is he still on water or has he decided to join the rest of us in a beer or something?"

What was it about the thought of Jack that made him want to argue?

"He thinks we drink too much," she said, "that we don't have our own lives. This weekly thing of seeing each other, barbecuing, and just being together seems excessive to him. At the same time, he's well aware I'm not asking his permission to have a glass of wine. And we're not talking about me and Jack, anyway. This is about that little girl in there. What are you going to do? Just so you know, Reine called me from that jail after you left, so I already knew. She's serious, Marcus. It's not that she's going to cut Eva out. She wants to know her, but at this point, her release is a long way down the road, and she's not seeing that far ahead right now. She doesn't know what's going to happen, but she wants—no, needs to know that Eva will have some permanence right now."

"So you're saying we should adopt her." He didn't pull his gaze from Karen, who, instead of taking another swallow of her wine, rested it on the porch beside her and then linked her hands together.

"I'm saying that right now, Reine's main concern is making sure there's something permanent for Eva. She's just trying to survive, and her dad has made some noise about taking Eva. I think she fears that he'll do it and she won't be able to stop him from where she is. I know only what she's shared with me about him, but he's volatile at times, or he was. He has another life now, and although he's changed some, she said much about him is the same, and she doesn't want Eva to ever feel as smothered as she did or to have to choose as she did. You and Charlotte have done amazing with Eva. Let me ask you this: Have you given any thought to five years down the road? Eva will be eleven when her mother is out. What would you do, just let her show up and take Eva? She won't be a little girl anymore. She's already part of our family. Would you just let her go?"

What was it about that question? He knew it was on everyone's mind, and it haunted him. He'd pushed the thought from his mind so many times, because he couldn't imagine just letting her go. He went to reach for the beer he didn't have and instead rested his hands on the arms of the wooden deck chair.

"I haven't let myself go there—which you know is something I don't do. I can't imagine her not being with us. Maybe it's changed since I said we'd take her. I never thought she'd steal a piece of my heart. I watch Charlotte with her, reading to her every night, helping her with counting, letters, printing, everything a first-grader does. She started school here. She's always with one of us or with Mom when we're working. I know she counts on us, but I also know this will crush her, not being able to see Reine. Will we adopt her? I can't believe you'd ask that. Is it even a question? Of course we will. It's done. What I don't understand is why Reine feels the need to cut her out completely and not see her. Eva looks forward to those visits. She's her mother still, no matter whether we adopt her. When we do, I'm the one who's going to have to tell Eva, and I haven't figure out how yet. She'll be crushed."

Karen was giving him everything. Something in those O'Connell blue eyes of hers held so many secrets. "You know what, Marcus? I know you'll figure out what to say. If you want us there, you know you just have to ask—but I agree with you on Reine. Maybe she will change her mind down the road, but right now she's doing the best she can in an impossible situation, making a decision she believes is the best thing for Eva. That's not a mother who's being selfish. She loves her daughter so much that she can see that you and Charlotte can give her more, give her the family she wants for her.

"I don't know what to say, Marcus, except she's made up her mind, maybe out of fear, maybe out of a whole lot of something else. She hasn't had a lot of say in so much in her life, having everything taken from her, but with Eva, with this, she does. All we can do is let her know how Eva's doing, keep in touch with her. From what she said to me when I talked to her, I know this isn't a decision she came to lightly. Then there's Charlotte. You figure out what you want there?"

He looked out into the darkness, hearing the squeak of the door, seeing Charlotte poke her head out, taking in him and Karen.

"We should get going, Marcus," she said. "Eva's tired. This has been a long day for her. I want to get her to bed. Alison asked if she can tag along and stay over."

Karen touched his hand, reached for her glass, and stood up. "And that's my cue," she said. "I'll leave you two and grab my husband. Seems like a good time for all of us to head home."

He took in Charlotte as Karen walked around her and rested a hand on her arm before stepping inside the house. When Charlotte walked over to him, he reached out his hand, and she rested hers in his. He pulled her onto his lap, and she settled in, resting her head on his shoulder.

"Yeah, probably a good idea," Marcus said. "How's she doing in there?"

Charlotte rested her hand on his, linking their fingers

together, and she seemed to really settle in. "She's good, laughing. Seems your family really knows how to chase away the shadows that linger after she sees her mom. So what do you want to do?"

He knew what she was asking. Of course, she'd been as thrown as he was when he told her what Reine had said. "I guess I want to face some things I've been putting off."

She pushed away from him and sat up, sitting on his lap still. He could see she was waiting for him to finish, her hands pressed against his chest. "And that means what, exactly? Just so you know, that little girl means everything to me. I want to adopt her. Just the thought of losing her when Reine is released... I wouldn't even admit it to myself, but I didn't want to give her up. I never told you, but I'm telling you now. I want to adopt her, Marcus. I know you don't want the forever thing with me..."

"Whoa, wait! I never said that," he said, running his hand up her arm. "Just so you know, I don't have commitment issues. I just needed to figure some stuff out. And you're not alone on the Eva front. I feel the same way. But first, I want to ask you something."

The way she was looking at him, he could see she was both suspicious and curious. "Okay, what?"

"Well, we'll adopt Eva and make that official, but first, we should make us official."

This time, she frowned, and he could feel her stiffen. "Are you saying...?"

"Yeah, I'm saying I think we should get married."

Her expression was priceless. "What changed?" she asked.

He had somehow moved her off his lap so he could stand, and he looked down at her as he rested his hands on her face. Then he pressed a kiss to her lips and got down on one knee.

"Charlotte, I love you. I love our family. Marry me. You're right. Let's make everything official, get it in writing, on paper."

She seemed to consider something for a second, but when she opened her mouth to speak, nothing came out. It was as if she didn't believe him or something.

"Charlotte, would you hurry up? The wood of this porch is digging into my knee, and it's damn uncomfortable."

"Of course I'll marry you," she said, and she helped him up.

He realized then, as he stood, that his family had been watching from the window. He just shook his head, pulled Charlotte into his arms, and kissed her.

Chapter 6

He took in the simple gold band on his ring finger. His tie was now long gone, along with his black suit jacket. His white shirtsleeves were rolled up, and the top two buttons of his shirt were undone as he leaned against the oak tree in the backyard of the house he'd grown up in.

"So you're pretty quiet over here, off by yourself," Owen said. "Is this regret at jumping into marriage too fast, and now you're asking yourself what you were thinking?"

His brother wore a suit, which was something he never did. It seemed no one was wearing a tie anymore, opting for comfort even though the ladies all still looked classy. Even Marcus's dark hair had been freshly cut. He took in his brothers, his family, the friends they'd invited to this backyard wedding. Even the justice of the peace, who had gone to school with Karen, was now deep in discussion with her.

"Yeah, just taking everything in, taking a minute,

figuring things out. I noticed you came alone and didn't bring a plus-one."

Owen gave nothing away. His face was poker straight, and Marcus wondered now if what Alison had said about him having girl trouble with some waitress was even true.

"Why would I?" he said. "Besides, this is you and Charlotte's day. It has nothing to do with me. A small backyard family wedding… I never expected you to be the one jumping the broom, so to speak, throwing together this shindig in a week. Like, what's the rush? I know you were on the fence about this whole marriage commitment thing to begin with—or is there something else going on?" Owen gestured with his beer over to Charlotte, who looked gorgeous in a sleeveless chiffon wedding dress as she stood laughing with Jenny and Suzanne. The wedding was for her. Then there was Eva, who was sitting with Alison on the patio swing, both in dresses, one blue, one peach. He'd even seen her laugh and smile a few times that day.

He just shook his head, lifted his own beer, and took a swallow.

Owen continued. "I hear them talking. They don't think I'm listening when I'm at the grill, and they do seem to share everything. Charlotte wanted to be married, but Jenny likes the status quo, just living under the same roof. She's carrying a lot of baggage, she'll be the first to admit to everyone, from her marriage with Wren. The control, the power… She knows Ryan isn't like that, but still. Then there's Suzanne and Harold, playing house at his place—and Karen? Well, she's as closed as you."

He wasn't sure what to make of Owen. He was shocked at how he knew all this and had never let on.

"So how'd Charlotte convince you, and so quickly?" Owen said.

What was he supposed to say to his brother? It had

been about his family, Charlotte and Eva, even though having that piece of paper, that kind of formality, still didn't sit right in ways he couldn't have explained.

"Who says she did?" he said. "You think anyone can convince me to do something if I don't want to do it?"

He shook his head as he took in Ryan and Luke both coming their way. Luke had arrived home just the day before from someplace overseas. His suit pulled at his buff frame, and his long dark hair was pulled back in a ponytail. The beard he'd sported was now gone.

"So this is what you want, then?" Owen added.

"Who wants what?" Ryan said. "What are we talking about here?"

Luke was still looking over his shoulder, checking everything and everyone out as if waiting for the unexpected to happen.

"Owen is just sticking his nose in my business, questioning my choices, asking if I'm really committed and why I suddenly gave in and got married—instead of focusing on himself," Marcus said. "But I'll tell you all the way of it: I love her, and she wants this. Makes no difference to me, but it's important to Charlotte. This was the forever thing for me, anyway, married or not. Then there's Eva, adopting her. It just seemed the right thing after what happened with Reine. I have no regrets, if that's what you're getting at, but at the same time, marriage is kind of about saying you're going to stick around and look after your family…"

His brothers exchanged a look. Of course, they had to have an idea of what he was getting at.

"So you're saying this thing about wanting to get married was about Dad?" Ryan said.

Meanwhile, Luke didn't pull his gaze from him.

Marcus wasn't sure what he was thinking, but with Luke, it could've been anything.

He took in his family, the woman he loved and the little girl who was quietly sitting with Alison, who he knew was doing her best to cheer her up. His teenage niece had her own baggage that had tested all of them.

"Well, we never knew there was trouble with Mom and Dad," Marcus said. "One day, he was just gone without a word. We never heard from him again. It kind of says, why bother having a family if you're going to just walk? So, evidently, the marriage thing didn't stop Dad from walking out the door and never coming back. You're right that to me it's just a piece of paper. It doesn't mean anything, considering the example he left…"

As Marcus trailed off, Owen seemed to hesitate and looked away. He couldn't read anything from him. Then there was Luke, who had written the book on holding his cards close to his chest. Ryan was shaking his head. Bringing up their dad was something they rarely did.

"Look, forget Dad," Ryan said. "He forgot us. I can't believe you've let anything of what he did affect what goes on between you and Charlotte. Yeah, he left." Ryan shrugged. "His loss."

"So what about Eva?" Owen said. "She knows you're adopting her? How is she doing?"

At the way his brother had shut down the topic, Marcus realized Owen never really did talk about their dad. Not that any of them did, but Owen never went there. At the same time, what could he tell his family about Eva? He didn't have a clue how to explain to her that life could be damn cruel sometimes.

"She's devastated," he said. "What do you want me to say? We should've been on the road to see her mom this morning, but Reine was serious. She won't see her, won't see us. Does Eva understand?" He just shook his head. "No. How could she when I don't understand it myself?"

"So you told that little girl her mama doesn't want to see her again?" Luke said. "You didn't try to be gentle or maybe tell her something that wasn't so cruel?"

Marcus knew his brother was rough around the edges, and he wasn't sure what to make of something that sounded like an accusation. "No, I told her the truth. She may be six, but I'm not going to start lying to her. What would I say, anyway, about why she can't see her mother? If I told her that Charlotte and I decided she couldn't see her, she'd never forgive us. She'd be angry, and who could blame her?"

"So now she's angry at her mother," Luke said, and he wasn't sure why he was sounding so pissed off.

"No, she isn't," Marcus snapped. "Charlotte and I sat her down and told her the truth, that her mom loves her so much that she doesn't want her to see her in jail, that it hurts her to have Eva come in and see her in a place like that, a bad, horrible place. We told her it's going to be a long time before she's out, and she wants us to adopt her so she can always be with us. We made sure she understood that in no way are we cutting her mother out of her life. We'll keep trying to reach out, and Reine wants to know how she's doing. I promised her I would keep in touch with her and let her know, but for now, she wouldn't see us or her. It may hurt, but lying to her or not telling her the whole truth would've been worse."

He wasn't sure his brothers agreed. He glanced over to Charlotte, who was walking their way. "Truth be told, Charlotte and I hadn't considered the end game, what would happen when Reine got out. It was haunting both of us. We'd never have been able to give her up. Is this good that this happened?" He just shook his head.

Charlotte stepped around Luke, who smiled and said, "Hey there, the new Mrs. O'Connell." He kissed her cheek, and she laughed.

"Thanks, Luke," she said, then slid her arm around Marcus. "Hey, your mom wants us. She's ordered a big cake and wants us to cut it for everyone."

His brothers had already walked away. He took in Suzanne in a purple dress and Karen in a red one with heels. Eva and Alison were setting the cake on the table, and his mom was directing Jack to shove more beers into a bucket of ice.

"How's Eva doing?" he asked. She'd been with Charlotte and his sisters all day, ever since they'd gotten dressed at home and driven over to his mom's for the wedding. She'd asked only once that morning whether they could see her mom. It still killed him to say they couldn't.

"Oh, she'll be okay. She's got your family and us. She'll likely keep asking about Reine, though. She was crying earlier inside, talking to Alison. By the way, Jenny has already insisted that Eva stay over with them tonight, considering it's our wedding night. Then Monday, we're back to work."

What could he say? He was the sheriff, and now wasn't the time to take off someplace for a honeymoon.

"You okay not going anywhere?" he asked.

She made a face and rested her palm on his chest, rubbing. She pressed her curves into him as she shook her head. "No, I'd rather be here. Besides, it wouldn't be good for Eva. She needs stability, and we need to have your sister get the papers started for the adoption. Then there's the other news I wanted to share with you."

He made a face, considering he didn't have a clue what she was talking about. "And that would be?"

"Oh, the fact that I'm pregnant, six weeks, so…"

For second, he didn't know what to say. "So we're having a baby?"

She allowed a smile to touch her lips. "We're having a baby," she said.

He held her in front of him and slid his arms over her shoulders, then lowered his head and pressed a kiss to her lips. He let it linger. "Marriage, adoption, and now a baby on the way... Wow, you're full of surprises, Charlotte Roy."

She cleared her throat and tapped his wrist. "O'Connell, in case you forgot. Charlotte O'Connell." She didn't try to hide the love she had for him.

He heard his family calling them.

"Well, we'd better go over there. So who do we tell first, everyone now, or...?"

"Eva," Charlotte said. "We'll tell her first, and then we'll tell your family."

And they started across the yard, his arm in hers.

Turn the page for a sneak peek of
THE MISSING FATHER
Available in print, eBook & audio

The Missing Father

The O'Connell family collides with danger in this shocking new story from *NY Times* and *USA Today* bestselling author Lorhainne Eckhart.

Eighteen years ago, Luke O'Connell's father was there one day, gone the next. His mother sat him and his siblings down and told them their father was gone, it was just them now, and they wouldn't be seeing him again. But Luke never believed his father could just walk away from a family he'd said he loved. Now, from his role within a secretive military organization, he uses the intelligence he can access to follow leads on his father, but each is a dead end.

Luke finds himself endlessly embroiled in deadly missions from secret bases, posing as a civilian for front companies, and tracking national enemies to capture or kill. But now, his questions have brought trouble back with him onto US soil, all the way to his hometown—and ultimately, his quest might put his family in the line of fire.

The Missing Father
CHAPTER 1

"So what you're saying is our target is a whistleblower?" said Master Sergeant Rex Barnes. "The man grew a pair and exposed a corrupt billion-dollar lab linked to our government, and our target isn't the company itself but the employee, who has now been named an enemy of the state? Just want to be sure I'm one hundred percent clear, here. This lab has been committing crimes against the public, fabricating crime scenes using DNA of their choosing, all with the blessing of the CIA, and we're saying this is okay? The operation was privately funded, yet now the technology is being sold to every rogue government and criminal, and we're meant to target the whistleblower who exposed the scheme? A man we once would've called a hero is now our enemy? Like, good God, what the hell has become of this country? Have we really been reduced to this?"

Master Sergeant Barnes was dark-haired and blue-eyed, hot-headed and ambitious, and at times he was confused for Luke, considering he had the same long dark hair tied back in a ponytail, the same broad shoulders, and the same height of six feet. Unlike Luke, though, Rex was grandstanding, as he usually did. He still hadn't learned the art of shutting his damn trap and keeping it shut in front of anyone in charge.

"It sounds to me as if you're challenging an order, Master Sergeant," said Colonel Raymond Powers. "Is there a problem here that I don't know about? Because last I heard, how this works is the orders come down from the White House, and you don't question them. It's not up to you to be the judge and jury and decide which assholes you shoot. The order comes down for your mission, I outline it, and you shut the fuck up and follow it. We don't get to question what falls under national security and what doesn't. You're a grunt. You pick up the gun and shoot who we tell you to."

Colonel Powers was the shortest member of the team, in his fifties, a retired operator on his third wife. He was standing at the end of the boardroom table in the command center where they were being briefed, wearing green fatigues and the same pissed-off, unsmiling expression he always had. "Sergeant Major, you need a minute with your team to see they have their heads screwed on straight?" he snapped at Jess Parker, the team leader.

Jess was perched on the end of the table instead of sitting in a seat, and he still hadn't shaved since arriving back stateside three days earlier. His bushy reddish hair was shoulder-length, but his beard and mustache gave him a hillbilly biker look that wouldn't have made him seem out of place on *America's Most Wanted*. Added to that was the tattoo on his forearm, a skull and crossbones emblazoned with the words "Death before dishonor"—something that would've been frowned on in the regular military but was good for their unit.

The 77th Operational Delta, known as the Wardogs,

were a special forces team that didn't really exist, reporting directly to the White House, which was both good and bad. It had started because of the war on terror, but, as of late, they had been more focused on protecting the dirty side of business.

"Nope, we're good to go," Jess said. "Seems Barnes has forgotten his manners and how he's supposed to be seen and not heard, just like the child he is, in the presence of his commanding officers. Not to worry. He's figuring it out now that we're back stateside. Isn't that right?"

Jess gave everything to Rex, who only lifted his hands arrogantly and didn't say another word. There was just something about Jess, who'd run their team for six years. He garnered all their respect unconditionally, and he knew how to shut each of them down, take the heat, and keep them all alive.

"So you'll be wheels up in two hours. That will be all," the colonel said before striding out of the secure room on the base at Fort Bragg.

Luke swiveled in the old black leather chair, taking in the now closed door, before turning back toward Sergeant First Class Matthew Newman, sitting across from him in a white T-shirt and khakis. The newbie, at twenty-five, was eager to impress. He was from Nebraska, with hazel eyes and nice, silky, long dirty blond hair and a smile that could sweet-talk the pants off any woman. He could've passed for a surfer, Luke thought, and he always had a different woman on his arm. His eyes could flash with teasing one minute and be filled with the kind of look that would have any sane man running the other way the next.

"I'm with Rex on this one," Matthew said. "This isn't sitting too right, Jess, that someone could use my DNA to fabricate a crime scene while I'm on the other side of the world. Definitely leaves me with a cold chill."

"This is what you signed up for," Jess said. "You're a grunt. You're not paid to think. You follow orders, end of story. The Harris Group is one of the leading genetics companies, responsible for cutting-edge medical research that saves lives." He took in each one of them.

From the other end of the table, Shaun Grant, Sergeant First Class, pitched in. "Doesn't it seem odd to you that we're being asked to go in and shut down this situation before it becomes known to the public? Seems as if more and more, we're becoming hired thugs." His black hair was close cropped, and he had dark skin and dark eyes, the biggest member of the team, at six foot two and likely three hundred pounds of solid muscle. His conference room chair seemed too small for his big frame. To Luke, Shaun was the one they all looked to, who had their backs and was always first through the door.

"So let me get this straight," Rex started again. "We're flying to Switzerland to capture a whistleblower, an executive at a private genetics lab funded by every government worldwide, which is stockpiling DNA from private citizens for all kinds of nefarious means in the name of research and development. He's exposed them for working with the CIA and other countries to manipulate DNA evidence and engineer crime scenes, and he's also exposed our government and the Harris Group for selling their technology to the highest bidder.

"But because he's stepped on the wrong toes and just because our government can, we're supposed to be okay with capturing this poor schmuck? He's the one being screwed here, in my opinion. We're going to toss him away in a hole forever, no trial, no nothing, because he sounded the alarm? This technology could result in any one of us being locked up forever on charges for a crime we didn't commit. Sounds to me like we're on the wrong side of this one."

Luke had long past realized that an order was an order. He'd lost track of the number of missions that had strayed into the corporate world that the government had its hands in. The wrong side was the wrong side, but the lines had started to blur.

"It's not up to us to question it," Jess said, looking around at them. "You know that. We take the order, and you do your job. You don't get an opinion. Are we clear here, or does anyone else have something to get off his chest before we're wheels up?"

To Luke, the five-member team were like his brothers. His family back in Livingston would likely have a serious fit if they knew what really went on behind the scenes in their government, if they knew about the kinds of assholes he was protecting.

"No, fine," Shaun said in his deep voice. "My mama always raised me to believe that honesty is the best policy, but scheming and dishonesty seem to be what we're defending now. Makes perfect sense to me." He was dressed in fatigues and a tan T-shirt. When he swiveled around in his chair, Luke sensed he seemed moodier than usual.

"Great, so now that we're all clear, remember this isn't a sanctioned military operation," Jess said. "We're going in as civilians. Know that this isn't sitting right with me, either, but we don't get to pick and choose our missions. We follow orders. That's what we signed on for. You'll need your suits for this one. Speaking of, Luke, how was your brother's wedding? How's your family?"

Luke could just make out Jess's blue eyes as the man lifted the shades he'd worn inside, something the colonel also never busted him for. But then, they were Jess's team, and they operated under an anonymity that Luke had once appreciated. The things they did wouldn't sit right with members of the regular army.

"He's married, but I'm not sure he buys into it, considering he's still stuck on the fact that our dad ditched us as kids," Luke said. "I didn't know it still bothered him, even though it fucked us all around. But hey, he did it. He's adopting the little girl, too, and I heard before leaving yesterday that he's going to be a baby daddy. Charlotte's preggers."

"Marcus is married, adopting that kid, and now about to be a father? Good for him. I'm happy for him," Rex said, jumping in, all smiles. "Has to make your mom happy."

Luke just took in his team, who'd met his family only a handful of times but knew everything about them and then some. They all knew more about each other and their issues, their secrets, than their own families knew.

Then everyone was up and started to the door, ready to hit their lockers and grab their bags, their guns, everything they'd need.

"Luke, got a second?" Jess added before he could leave.

"Sure," he said, realizing it was only him and Jess left in the conference room.

"Just wanted to give you a heads-up that the lead you asked Sienna to follow up on, the one about Raymond O'Connell, turned up nothing. Yes, Sienna was under the impression that I knew about the request. When she mentioned it to me, I knew the man had to be your dad, and I thought, 'Now, what the hell is Luke doing?' So now I'm asking, why are you having Sienna Parker, our CIA agent, look for your dad?"

In that moment, Luke wanted nothing more than to pull Sienna aside and ask her what the hell she was doing.

"You've known me a long time," Luke said. "Fine, here it is. There's just something about the fact that my father up and walked away from his family eighteen years ago that's never sat right with me. We never heard from him again, and from what I've figured out, he vanished into thin air. Now, who does that? We have the resources, so yeah, I've been doing some homework. You going to bust me for that?"

Jess glanced over to the door and back to him, but he didn't say anything for another second. "Cut the crap, Luke. You can't have Sienna doing personal investigating for you. Your dad evidently doesn't want to be found—but then again, there could be another option."

"You mean that he could be dead?" Luke said. That was the thing he'd thought of over and over. If his father had disappeared and walked away, he was either dead or didn't want to be found. "If he's dead, how is it that I can't find anything on him? The more I dig, the more holes I find."

Jess ran his hand over his chin. "Well, then maybe you have your answer." He started to the door before turning back to him. "Luke, if you keep digging, the answers you find may not be the ones you want. Oh, and one more thing," Jess said, his hand on the door. "Consider this your birthday present, me coming to you. Sienna's doing you this favor, but then she came to me. You may want to ask yourself, what is she up to?"

Click here to order your copy and keeping reading.

About the Author

"Lorhainne Eckhart is one of my go to authors when I want a guaranteed good book. So many twists and turns, but also so much love and such a strong sense of family."

(Lora W., Reviewer)

New York Times & USA Today bestseller Lorhainne Eckhart writes Raw Relatable Real Romance is best known for her big family romances series, where "Morals and family are running themes. Danger, romance, and a drive to do what is right will see you glued to the page." As one fan calls her, she is the "Queen of the family saga." (aherman) writing "the ups and downs of what goes on within a family but also with some suspense, angst and of course a bit of romance thrown in for good measure." Follow Lorhainne on Bookbub to receive alerts on New Releases and Sales and join her mailing list at LorhainneEckhart.com for her Monday Blog, books news, giveaways and FREE reads. With over 120 books, audiobooks, and multiple series published and available at all retailers now translated into six languages. She is a multiple recipient of the Readers' Favorite Award for Suspense and Romance, and lives in the Pacific Northwest on an island, is the mother of three, her oldest has autism and she is an advocate for never giving up on your dreams.

"Lorhainne Eckhart has this uncanny way of just hitting the spot every time with her books."

The O'Connells: *The O'Connells of Livingston, Montana are not your typical family. A riveting collection of stories surrounding the ups and downs of what goes on within a family but also with some suspense, angst and of course a bit of romance thrown in for good measure "I thought I loved the Friessens, but I absolutely adore the O'Connell's. Each and every book has totally different genres of stories but the one thing in common is how she is able to wrap it around the family which is the heart of each story." (C. Logue)*

The Friessens: *An emotional big family romance series, the Friessen family siblings find their relationships tested, lay their hearts on the line, and discover lasting love! "Lorhainne Eckhart is one of my go to authors when I want a guaranteed good book. So many twists and turns, but also so much love and such a strong sense of family." (Lora W., Reviewer)*

The Parker Sisters: *The Parker Sisters are a close-knit family, and like any other family they have their ups and downs. "Eckhart has crafted another intense family drama…The character development is outstanding, and the emotional investment is high…" (Aherman, Reviewer)*

The McCabe Brothers: *Join the five McCabe siblings on their journeys to the dark and dangerous side of love! An intense, exhilarating collection of romantic thrillers you won't want to miss. — "Eckhart has a new series that is definitely worth the read. The queen of the family saga started this series with a spin-off of her wildly successful Friessen series." From a Readers' Favorite award—winning author and "queen of the family saga" (Aherman)*

Lorhainne loves to hear from her readers! You can connect with me at:
www.LorhainneEckhart.com
lorhainneeckhart.le@gmail.com

Also by Lorhainne Eckhart

The Outsider Series
The Forgotten Child (Brad and Emily)
A Baby and a Wedding *(An Outsider Series Short)*
Fallen Hero (Andy, Jed, and Diana)
The Search *(An Outsider Series Short)*
The Awakening (Andy and Laura)
Secrets (Jed and Diana)
Runaway (Andy and Laura)
Overdue *(An Outsider Series Short)*
The Unexpected Storm (Neil and Candy)
The Wedding (Neil and Candy)

The Friessens: A New Beginning
The Deadline (Andy and Laura)
The Price to Love (Neil and Candy)
A Different Kind of Love (Brad and Emily)
A Vow of Love, A Friessen Family Christmas

The Friessens
The Reunion
The Bloodline (Andy & Laura)
The Promise (Diana & Jed)
The Business Plan (Neil & Candy)
The Decision (Brad & Emily)
First Love (Katy)
Family First
Leave the Light On
In the Moment
In the Family

The Stalker
The O'Connell Family Christmas

The McCabe Brothers
Don't Stop Me (Vic)
Don't Catch Me (Chase)
Don't Run From Me (Aaron)
Don't Hide From Me (Luc)
Don't Leave Me (Claudia)
Out of Time

A Billy Jo McCabe Mystery
Nothing As it Seems
Hiding in Plain Sight
The Cold Case

The Wilde Brothers
The One (Joe and Margaret)
The Honeymoon, A Wilde Brothers Short
Friendly Fire (Logan and Julia)
Not Quite Married, A Wilde Brothers Short
A Matter of Trust (Ben and Carrie)
The Reckoning, A Wilde Brothers Christmas
Traded (Jake)
Unforgiven (Samuel)
The Holiday Bride

Married in Montana
His Promise
Love's Promise
A Promise of Forever

The Parker Sisters
Thrill of the Chase

The Dating Game
Play Hard to Get
What We Can't Have
Go Your Own Way
A June Wedding

Kate & Walker
One Night
Edge of Night
Last Night

Walk the Right Road Series
The Choice
Lost and Found
Merkaba
Bounty
Blown Away: The Final Chapter

The Saved Series
Saved
Vanished
Captured

Single Titles
He Came Back
Loving Christine

For my German Readers
Die Außenseiter-Reihe
Der Vergessene Junge
Der Gefallene Held

For my French Readers
L'ENFANT OUBLIÉ

CPSIA information can be obtained
at www.ICGtesting.com
Printed in the USA
BVHW031051110821
614177BV00007B/228